Soul Love

Lynda Waterhouse lives in Elephant and Castle in South London. Her hobbies include missing aerobics classes, watching silent movies and listening to anti-folk music.

Soul Love

LYNDA WATERHOUSE

Piccadilly Press • London

First published in Great Britain in 2004
by Piccadilly Press Ltd,
5 Castle Road, London NW1 8PR
www.piccadillypress.co.uk

A catalogue record for this book is available from the British Library

ISBN: 185340 860 3 (trade paperback)

1 3 5 7 9 10 8 6 4 2

Printed and bound in Great Britain by Bookmarque Ltd

Cover design and illustration by Susan Hellard
Text design by Louise Millar

Set in Sabon and Regular Joe

To my soul love, D.H.

Prologue

It's a warm summer's evening. The Saturday of the August bank holiday weekend, to be precise. The stars have never looked so bright. I'm sitting at my bedroom window, staring up at the dazzling display, and I'm thinking about what happened to me that summer.

What a different person I, Jenna Hudson, was then.

Remembering hurts. My brain tries to locate exactly where the pain is, but soon gives up because I hurt all over.

I'm fed up of being grown-up and mature about my life. I want to be a child again – a six-year-old girl who's fallen off her bike. I want to screw my face up, scream loudly and run wailing into the kitchen where my mum would gather me up tight in her arms and kiss the scrape on my knee better. Then I'd stop crying and sip chocolate milk until the pain eased.

That's one thing about growing up they don't tell you – dealing with the sort of pain that can't be kissed away.

Chapter One

I breathed a huge sigh of relief when the car turned into the road leading to Aunt Sarah's cottage. When we'd set off from London, Mum and I weren't speaking so I had no idea where she was going to dump me. Given the mood she was in, she would have been quite capable of buying me a one-way ticket to boot camp, where I'd have spent the summer holidays dressed in a brown sack and only being allowed to say, 'Yes, sir! No, sir!'

'I can't hang about, Jenna,' Mum said in a sharp voice as she opened the car boot and deposited my bags on the tarmac. 'Marcus frets if I'm away too long.'

I groaned. There was no way I was going to break my no-speaking rule yet. I was too mad at her for that. Typical that she'd be worrying more about my little eight-year-old brother than me. I just rolled my eyes and stayed in the car as she walked up to Aunt Sarah's cottage.

From the back Mum could be mistaken for a teenager. It never ceased to amaze me. Her long hair was scrunched up into a funky ponytail and she was wearing kitten heels. From the front, however, it was a different story these days. Her face was one big permanent scowl. And it was all down to me. According to her, my behaviour over the last few months had aged her ten years.

She should consider herself lucky. When Tara Cowley's mum discovered that Tara had failed all her exams on purpose, her hair had turned white overnight. What I had done was much worse than failing a few exams and Mum's hair was still the same shiny nut-brown.

All I heard from my mum in the days before we'd stopped speaking was, 'Jenna, how could you . . .' or that all-time classic, 'When I was your age, Jenna . . .', followed by the 'modern-parent' grumble, 'Do you know how hard it was to get you into Coot's Hill School in the first place? I had to buy this hideous house just because it was in the catchment area!'

I did feel a bit bad about that. Good schools are hard to get into in London.

Mum would then begin muttering about having to go private – 'If they'd take you!'

When I heard, 'Jenna, when I was your age . . .' for the trillionth time, I snapped.

'But Mum, that was in the dark ages when fifteen-year-old girls wore big frilly knickers and got excited by hockey and iced buns!'

Then we had a massive row and stopped speaking to each other altogether.

What else could I do? Hadn't I promised Mia I wouldn't tell? And hadn't *Mum* always drilled into me how important it was to keep promises? As I was leaving my house I'd seen Mia looking down at me from her bedroom window across the road. She was dressed in her school uniform. She just kept staring at me and I looked away.

I glared out of the car window as Mum talked to Sarah. They both turned and looked at me. I continued glaring. Mum frowned back and Sarah gave me a weak smile. Mum began to talk animatedly, waving her arms about. No doubt telling her all the gory details about how her only daughter managed to get herself excluded from 'such a good' school.

Actually, I hadn't been expelled. Technically, I was leaving two weeks before the end of the summer term to 'make a fresh start'. But Mrs Kelly, the head teacher, had made it perfectly clear that I was no longer welcome at Coot's Hill.

The thought of all those embarrassing meetings in her office made me shudder. So I dug myself deeper into my seat, where, for the moment, it was safe and warm. I looked in the rear-view mirror, and imagined myself in an American police drama. I put on my meanest expression as a cop read out my description. 'Single, white female; five foot, four inches tall; long, red/brown hair with blond streaks, green eyes, squidgy nose and fat lips. Refuses to talk. Yup, this one's a real *bad* girl.'

Obviously the 'bad girl' story had another side to it. There was a part of me that wanted to just break down and tell Mum everything. To be fair, she had tried to get it out of me. I couldn't even bring myself to think about what I'd done without feeling sick to my stomach. To be honest, the fall-out with Mum was really just a smokescreen. It meant that I didn't have to talk to her about it. She had even rung up Dad and told him and my stepmum all about it. I came close to cracking several times. But then there was Mia. How could I let her down?

Mum had kept on and on asking, 'Did Mia put you up to it?' It was always the same question in a hundred different variations.

I hated the way she assumed that only another child could be blamed for such unexpected behaviour. 'I'm not a child. I can make my own decisions,' I had said over and over again. I had a right to keep some things to myself. Plus, she was getting too close to the truth.

Mum startled me out of my thoughts as she wrenched the car door open. 'Get out, Jenna.'

I got out as slowly as I could whilst Mum and Sarah gave each other a hug goodbye.

Sarah was Mum's older sister, but she looked younger. 'No career and no kids to age her!' Mum had said once, with a tinge of resentment in her voice.

'Are you sure you won't stay for a cup of tea?' Sarah asked in her soft voice.

Mum shook her head. 'No, I'm too wound up. I'll stop off at the motorway services.'

'Jenna.' She spoke to the air above my head. 'I've given Sarah some money for your keep.'

I stuck my hands in my jeans pockets and shrugged my shoulders. After she had driven off down the road I raised my hand into an ironic wave and said, 'Bye, Mum. Love you too!'

So, I had been exiled to Aunt Sarah's. My job was to have a miserable summer and be grateful when Her Majesty said I could return to a new school in London.

Chapter Two

Sarah lived in a small terraced cottage in a back-of-beyond, middle-of-nowhere village called Little Netherby, slap bang in the middle of the nothingness that's called the countryside. A place where old folks go for mind-numbingly boring holidays and where mothers send their newly minted bad girls to get them away from the influences of city living.

She lived there with her partner, Kai, and her cat, Tallulah.

Sarah and Kai owned a second-hand bookshop in the next village, Greater Netherby. They were both poets who did readings at festivals or in dark, empty rooms above smoky, city pubs. Mum, Mia and I had gone along to one of their readings the previous summer in an 'alternative' café in South London. Sarah's poems were really funny, but she read them out in a small voice with lots of nervous tics so it almost felt like she was apologising for herself.

Kai's poems were toe-curlingly, teeth-achingly bad. They were long rants, full of stuff about naked bodies, human smells and the power of lust. Old gals Mum's age seemed to lap it up, swooning over his 'rock star' looks and so-called 'ability to understand women'. Mia and I had got seriously glared at for giggling at his poems. Mum had commanded that we 'grow up', which had just made us giggle even more.

I chucked my bags down in the tiny hall and went inside the cottage. It was like walking into a junk shop. Every available space was crammed with stuff. I had to blink several times to clear my vision, as books, boxes, pieces of decorative fabric and hideous pottery all fought for my attention.

'Kai's away on a book-buying trip,' Sarah said brightly as she brushed away a strand of wispy dark hair from her face. She had silver rings on every finger and hundreds of jangly bracelets on her arms. Every time she moved she sounded like a wind charm in a gale. 'Are you OK?' she asked as I stood in the centre of the room, blinking madly.

Before I could answer she moved into the kitchen and started rattling some cups around. She said, 'I don't know about you, but I'm gasping for a coffee.'

I grunted and flopped down on the dusty sofa and got ready to watch some TV. Instead, I found myself staring into the eyes of a large black cat sitting in the space where the TV should've been. We blinked at each other for a few moments before she launched herself off the table and landed with a thud on my lap. She then began to purr loudly.

Sarah came back in with two large mugs and laughed. 'Tallulah must like you if she's doing her industrial purring. My cat is not easily impressed. She goes where she pleases and does what she likes. She often comes with me to the shop.'

I took a sip of coffee and cut to the chase. 'How long am I here for?'

Sarah sighed and tugged at her hair again before replying. 'For the holidays . . . to begin with. Then there's a new school to sort out. There's always Netherby Community School if you want a fresh start away from the city.' She sat down beside me and stroked Tallulah. After a long pause she went on, 'Look, Jenna, you are grown-up enough to know that I can't force you to do anything. I can't make you tell me what really happened at school and I can't make you stay here. I'm not your jailor. I don't want to be. You can walk out of here any time you like. All that I ask is that you let me know first.'

That stunned me, because in the car on the way down I'd been planning a big speech along the lines of: 'You can't keep me here. I'll run away. You can't make me do anything!' Then I'd planned to lapse into silence, just like with Mum. I was going to keep schtum until Mia, in the form of some weird fairy godmother, set me free with the truth.

There was even a name for my condition. I'd found it in Mum's dictionary of adolescent problems, which was conveniently left lying around the kitchen. It was called Elective Mutism. Or in my case, Selective Mutism.

Sarah's speech had left me *truly* speechless. I drank my coffee and allowed myself to feel a bit more cheerful. The place felt less like a prison if it was my choice whether I stayed or not.

'Can I use the phone?' I asked. Mum had confiscated my mobile.

Sarah spent ages fiddling with her bracelets before saying, 'Actually, the phone's been disconnected.'

For a second I felt pleased. It meant a break from Mum's nagging voice. Then it hit me. No TV, no telephone and no friends. No distractions and plenty of time to brood. Maybe a spell at boot camp wouldn't have been so bad after all.

Chapter Three

I opened the curtains the next morning to see a semi-naked body in a deck chair in next-door's back garden. I took a step back from the window and risked another peek.

I could make out a tight muscular torso with small brown nipples. His skin was startlingly pale. My eyes slowly traced a fine line of dark black hair from underneath the belly button to the top of his faded jeans. They continued along the line of his jeans pausing to take in the tear on one of the knees and the white toes that were rhythmically stroking the grass.

His face was hidden from view by the book he was reading. I watched and waited, hoping no one could see me. Every now and then his hand would scratch his chest or brush a fly away.

The door squeaked suddenly and I jumped away from the window. No one likes to be caught drooling, do they?

'Tallulah!' I sighed with relief as the cat padded in, looking for attention.

When I looked again, the boy had turned round and was pulling on a faded red T-shirt with his back towards me. I liked the way his dark black hair curled around his neck.

I smiled as Tallulah batted me with her paw and meowed crossly. Then I smiled again, because it had felt weird to be smiling. The only smiling that I'd been doing lately was of the joyless, laugh-out-loud, 'Ha! I don't give a damn' variety that made your face ache and your heart burn.

Tallulah weaved herself between my legs, head-butting my knees in order to get some attention. I was starving, too. Yesterday, Mum had been too mad at me to think about eating so I'd survived on chocolate bars bought during our service station stops. Last night I was too tired to be tempted by Sarah's offer of reheated mung bean curry, but now I could eat the entire contents of the fridge.

I looked out the window once more before heading to the kitchen. The deck chair was empty, apart from the book. Hadn't I sworn that I was going to have nothing to do with boys for at least a year? Liking boys had played a large part in the trouble Mia and I had got ourselves into. One boy in particular, but I wasn't going to think about Jackson now. I couldn't even bear to look at his photo, hidden away in my purse.

I found Sarah standing on her head in the lounge. She called out, 'Help yourself to breakfast!'

The kitchen was only marginally less dusty than the rest of the place. There was an assortment of cupboards, a grease-encrusted cooker and an ancient fridge. As I tugged the heavy door open the fridge rumbled and shook. Inside was half a carton of milk and some bean curd that looked more like green turd. Eating the entire contents of the fridge instantly lost its appeal.

There was a large shelf full of cookbooks, but the rest of the cupboards were empty. I found an old box of cereal and the milk didn't smell bad. I wandered out into the back garden to eat it. It was a lovely sunny morning and it wouldn't do any harm to check out Torso Boy some more from a better vantage point.

Sarah had maintained the 'neglect' theme into the small back garden. It was an overgrown tangle of weeds with a rusty car door right in the centre. I sat down on a wobbly wooden bench.

'Bit of a mess, isn't it?' Sarah said as she sat down next to me.

Your life or the garden? I thought to myself, but aloud I said, 'Isn't Kai into green things? His poems are all about nature, aren't they?'

Sarah started to laugh loudly. It startled me because the laugh didn't seem to belong to her. It belonged to a coarse loudmouth, not to my quiet, sensitive aunt. Then she gulped in some more air and said, 'Ha! You thought Kai was into green things, did you?'

I watched in horror as the huge belly laughs transformed themselves into floods of tears and she lunged at me. I had no idea how to deal with this, so I gave her back a few awkward pats as if she were some grotesque oversized baby.

After a painfully long time she said, 'Kai's left me.'

I was speechless again. This wasn't supposed to be happening. Sarah was supposed to be supporting and guiding *me*. I wasn't equipped to deal with her problems. The only thing that should have been on my mind was trying to see if Torso Boy's face was as cute as his body.

'He left me three weeks ago. Said he needed some creative space. He felt that my poetry was stale and that he turned into a vegetable whenever I walked into the room.'

I resisted asking the question, 'Carrot or courgette?' – even I knew that this wasn't the time for silly jokes. It would be hard for Sarah to see the funny side when someone you love had insulted you so badly. I nodded and made a sympathetic grunt.

Sarah blew her nose on a screwed-up piece of tissue and said, 'He took the TV, computer and most of our money. The phone has been cut off and I'm going out of my mind with worry wondering where he is.'

I made some more sympathetic noises, although I had to admit that part of me felt a tinge of pleasure at learning that I wasn't the only person in this family who had stuffed up. Mum was always going on at me about the bad choices that I was making. You didn't have to be Sherlock Holmes to figure out that Kai was not going to be Mr Reliable. All those poems about hunting for rare flowers in damp tropical forests and worshipping naked statues of goddesses were a bit of a give-away.

We sat in silence for a few moments. I tried not to make too much noise crunching my cereal. From time to time I glanced over at next door's garden. This was probably not the best time to ask about who lived there.

Sarah blew her nose again and continued. 'We didn't have children because he said that would kill off his creative spirit. He said that running Sarakai Books was enough of a distraction. I would have loved to have children. Came pretty close to persuading him once, but I respected his creativity. Kai's art comes first . . .'

The cereal turned to sawdust in my mouth. What could I say? I'd never seen an adult in this state before. My brain flapped around like a goldfish out of water until it came up with, 'Has he got someone else?'

My dad had left us for his PA before marrying a librarian called – I kid you not – Foxy. It was difficult at first, but now Mum's happy and Dad's happy. We get two dinners at Christmas. Result all round.

Sarah smiled at me. 'It's nothing as clichéd as that! I'm sure he'll come back. He never misses the Netherby Festival. He's always such a big hit there.'

'What is it?' I asked.

'You've never heard of the Netherby Festival? What *does* my sister talk to you about? It's only one of the most famous alternative festivals in the country. It takes place on the August bank holiday in the grounds of Netherby Hall. It's amazing. You'll have to go.'

I grunted unenthusiastically. I wasn't planning on sticking around that long. I was hoping to be back in London within the next couple of weeks.

Sarah sprang up and punched the air. 'What we need is some positive action!' she declared. 'When do we want it? NOW!'

We spent the rest of the morning hacking away at the weeds. After about an hour I 'casually' asked, 'What are the people next door like?'

'I've been really lucky with my neighbours. This terrace was originally built to house farm labourers so they are quite small and close together. Mr Gordon lives on that side, but he only uses the cottage at weekends. Evie Winthrope lives on the other side, but she's off on another of her jaunts to Africa so she's rented out her place to some college students for the summer. Freddie and Charlie live there at the moment. They're fun. The only thing they take seriously is their music. They are an anti-folk band.'

I had no idea what anti-folk was, but I just nodded my head. I wondered which one, Charlie or Freddie, I'd already seen. They might turn out to be company for the short time I was here in this weird summer.

At around twelve the sun was really beating down on us so we stopped working.

'Is there anything else I can do?' I asked.

Sarah tugged at her hair and said, 'You could go to Greater Netherby and open the shop up for me. The float is hidden in the old toffee tin under the counter and all the books are priced up. I'll join you later. Saturday is my busiest day.' She handed me a large set of keys and explained which ones opened what.

Mum never let me go to the shops without a list and strict instructions to give her all the change back. Was Sarah really asking me to *run* her shop for the day?

I felt the weight of the keys in my hand and I didn't say a word. At least I was being taken seriously.

Chapter Four

Greater Netherby was only a ten-minute walk from Little Netherby. It had one charity shop, a café, a chemist's, hairdresser's and the bookshop, which was tucked away on the corner at the bottom of the street, with just a small, hand-carved sign that said: *Sarakai Secondhand Books*. Blink and you'd miss it.

I fiddled with the keys to find the right one, trying to recall Sarah's instructions. As I struggled with the door I felt a prickly sensation on the back of my neck, as if a hundred pairs of eyes were watching me. The curtain in the hairdresser's window opposite twitched and two old ladies walked out of the charity shop to take a good long look at me before doubling back into the shop. This was not like London, where people don't care to know your business. Here, a stranger unlocking the bookshop was hot news.

I pushed past a wedge of post to get inside. The shop was much larger than it seemed from the outside. There was a counter to the left of the entrance and behind that was a small office space. Beyond the counter, the shop turned into a forest of shelves that seemed to stretch for miles and miles. Beside one of the bookcases was a tatty armchair. This place was so dusty it made Sarah's cottage seem like an operating theatre by comparison. I started to cough. This was not a place to work in if you had a dust allergy or delicate nerves. The badly fitted shelves groaned under the weight of books. It seemed like it would only take one false move or loud sneeze and the whole thing would collapse.

The only dust-free object was a shiny new poster advertising the Netherby Festival in August. I noted that there were some pretty cool bands playing.

On my way to fetch the float, I tripped over a box of old records, labelled: *Kai's personal property. NOT FOR SALE.* I gave the box an extra kick. How dare he say he turned into a vegetable every time Sarah walked into the room! It was a bit rich, coming from a man who transformed into a lecherous toad whenever anything remotely female entered a room.

I scooped up the mountains of post, plopped it all on the counter and took a look at the office space. It didn't take long. There was a cash register, an old computer, a grubby radio and a battered office chair, complete with an old velvet cushion that was covered in cat hair. There was also an ancient telephone made of heavy plastic. There was no dial tone, but at least the radio worked. I tuned it to an R'n'B music station. I took the cushion off the chair and swung round in my seat. On my second swing I encountered a mass of white whiskers and a pair of watery eyes looking back at me.

'You're new,' Whiskers said.

Without thinking, I answered, 'You're old.'

He burst out laughing and said 'Touché!' Then he held out his hand. 'Julius Lawrence, at your service! Everyone calls me Julius.'

'I'm Jenna,' I said, eyeing him cautiously.

Julius continued smiling and speaking in a loud voice. 'Ah,

Jenna. The girl with the green eyes! I used to own this fair establishment until I retired. It was called Julius Lawrence Antiquarian Books in my day. It specialised in books about art and photography then.' He fingered the straps of an old camera round his neck and went on. 'Many moons ago, I fancied myself as a bit of a photographer. Now like a faithful old Labrador, I keep coming back to my old hunting ground. It's come in very handy since they closed down the library. By the way there's some correspondence stuck in the door.'

I followed his gaze to where a crumpled brown envelope was jammed under the door.

'I guess that's why I didn't hear you come in,' I said.

He walked over to a shelf and pulled out a book that had a bookmark in it. Then he sat down in the armchair. 'Don't mind me. I'm what is known as a "local character".'

I turned the music up and tried to ignore him. Although I'd never admit it, I was actually quite glad of the company. I liked being treated like an adult, but it was scary to be left in charge of a shop – albeit a dusty old bookshop with a naff name.

Julius barked across the room, 'Sarah usually has Radio 4 on low. Music can be quite distracting when one is trying to lose oneself in a book.'

'You know what they say, Julius,' I yelled back at him, bending down to switch on the computer. I was hoping to send some e-mail to Mia and Jackson. '"Music hath charms to soothe the savage beast."'

Above me, a sparky voice said, '*Breast!* I think it's breast.'

I popped my head out from underneath the table and found myself staring at a familiar faded red T-shirt. I bobbed quickly back under the table.

'Er, breast,' I said as I struggled to banish thoughts of his naked chest from my mind. Then I banged my head as I backed out from underneath the table and into an ambush of cobwebs that had been hanging in wait for me.

By the time I had got to my feet he had walked over to a shelf, pulled out a book and handed it to me.

'"Music hath charms to soothe the savage breast,"' he said, then he nodded, turned and walked out of the shop, leaving me with a book of quotations in my hands and wearing a fetching cobweb headdress.

Not the most promising of introductions. Plus, I still hadn't really been able to take in what he looked like without a book in front of his face.

I dislodged the letter that was wedged under the door. I didn't want any more surprise visitors. To keep myself busy, I dug out a box of felt-tips from under the counter and added *Customers preferred!* to the tatty *Browsers welcome* sign. Then I sat back and began to relax.

About an hour later a loud ring shattered my calm.

'The bells! The bells!' Julius did a terrible Hunchback of Notre-Dame impression that he seemed to think was hilarious and I stared at the old lady who'd just walked in. With her purple hair and bright red lips, she looked like she belonged on the set of an ancient horror movie.

She plonked down a pile of books on the counter, pointed at my sign and said, 'I prefer customers myself. Mind you, you don't get as many time-wasters in the hairdresser's where I work.'

'I'm not buying today,' I said, eyeing the pile warily. I hadn't worked out how to use the cash register yet, and I didn't know if I was allowed to buy books.

'Aren't you? Well, I'm sure you know your business.' She went over to a shelf and began flicking through some tatty paperbacks.

Julius looked up. 'That's Ava. She's another regular.'

Ava straightened her brightly coloured cardigan. 'I'm quite capable of introducing myself, thank you very much, Julius.' She rolled her eyes. 'I expect Sarah has already briefed you about the Rampant Romantics.'

'*L'amour, toujours l'amour!*' Julius gushed.

Ava was still looking at me expectantly. 'The Rampant Romantics,' she repeated slowly, as if I were stupid. 'Sarah must have told you about us.'

'Not exactly,' I mumbled. 'I've only just arrived.'

'We have an arrangement. We circulate our romantic fiction around the village and the shop. If any should be sold in the shop then Sarah gets to keep the money.'

In a swift move she replaced the books on the shelf with her copies and whizzed the others into a string bag. She also put down a paper bag on the counter.

'I brought this in for Sarah. Is she feeling any better? She's got to eat. Heartbreak is a terrible thing.' She leaned in so close to me that I could smell her peppermint-flavoured breath. She grabbed hold of my arm and squeezed it tightly, saying, 'Mind you, I never quite trusted that Kai. He has a roving eye and a finely cut calf muscle. Mix that with a few rhyming couplets, and you've got a lethal combination.'

'People say I have good legs,' Julius cut in. He stood and rolled up his trouser leg.

Ava rolled her eyes again and said, 'I can't stand round chatting all day. I've got some heads to wash.' She wiggled out of the shop in her tight pencil skirt.

Julius watched her every move and whistled, 'What a woman!'

Another hour passed by and I was still struggling to get the computer to work when Julius got up from the chair and stretched.

'Would you care to join me for a spot of afternoon tea at the café?'

'No thanks. I'd better go and check on Sarah. She ought to have been here by now,' I mumbled. I wasn't in the mood for drinking tea with an old fogey.

'After tea I'll pop back and keep an eye on the shop for you. Sarah let me hang on to my set of keys,' he said.

When Julius had gone I peeped into the bag that Ava had left. Inside it was a large piece of bread and butter pudding. The sweet spicy smell was irresistible so I broke off a chunk, wolfed it down and went off in search of Sarah.

On my way back up the high street, I peeped into the café. I'd expected it to be one of those over-fussy tea shops with heavy-patterned wallpaper and lace tablecloths, but it had stripped pine tables and internet access. It was definitely worth checking out another time. I paused to brush a sugar crystal from my cheek and spotted Julius sitting in the window, waving his arms and chatting animatedly to none other than Torso Boy.

Just as I was about to walk away, the boy turned his head and caught my eye for a fraction of a second. It was like someone had dropped an ice cube down my back. I looked down and continued quickly on my way.

My mind buzzed. Why had I reacted like that? Why had I said I'd go and check on Sarah instead of going for tea with

Julius? If I hadn't, I might be getting to know Torso Boy. And why was I so bothered about that boy anyway? He probably treated girls like arm-candy like Jackson did. And when there was any real trouble around, he'd walk away too.

I slapped my head. One thing was certain. I would have to get him out of my mind, because I, Jenna Hudson, had an amazing ability to always make the wrong choice.

Chapter Five

Sarah had taken to her bed like a soppy romantic heroine in an historical drama. Her eyes were red raw with crying. She blew her nose loudly and said, 'Sorry I didn't make it to the shop. I just couldn't face it.'

'I had no idea where you were!' I replied. 'You could've let me know . . .' Then I checked myself. The phone was cut off, and I was sounding too much like Mum in nag-mode.

She grinned weakly. 'I'll see about getting the phone reconnected tomorrow.'

'I couldn't get the computer to boot up either,' I added.

Sarah's eyes misted over again. 'Kai has a knack for making it work.'

I quickly changed the subject. 'Have you eaten?' Sarah shook her head. I'd finished off the rest of the bread and butter pudding on the way home so I rustled us up some spaghetti with half a tin of tuna. Not exactly fine dining, but you can only work with what you've got. Tallulah got most of my half.

After that measly meal, I prised some of Mum's money from Sarah and went out. I had noticed a Mini-Mart in Little Netherby, which was about half a mile down the lane towards Greater Netherby.

As I walked there I made a mental note to ask Julius

tomorrow what the deal was with all these Netherbys. He'd be bound to know the local history of the place. I assumed that I'd be looking after the shop again. There was no way Sarah was in a fit state to run the place alone.

Mum would die of shock if she could see me volunteering to go to work, as well as doing the cooking and shopping. Thinking of Mum gave me a twinge of guilt followed by a huge wave of homesickness. There was a phone box outside the Mini-Mart. Maybe just a quick call would break the 'no speaking' mood that had ruined so much of the last few weeks.

To my surprise, the phone box was spotless inside. There were no junk food cartons or illegal chatline cards. I'm not sure why, but I found myself dialling Mia's number first.

Mia's mum answered. 'Is that you, Jenna?' Her voice sounded like she was trapped in a room full of bad smells.

'Yes, Mrs Andrews. I'm phoning from a call-box for a quick word with Mia.'

Mia's parents were investment bankers who left their house at six a.m. every morning with their personal trainers and usually got back home (after a power business dinner) at around ten p.m. Mia had housekeepers, a personal maths tutor, an au pair, plenty of money . . . and me to keep her company.

There was a long pause, then, 'Mia is round at the Worths' having some catch-up French tuition from Becky's private tutor.'

I bet Mia's loving that, I thought. She's always going on about how stuck-up Rebecca Worth is!

Mia's mum sighed and said, 'I really don't think that it is a good idea for you and Mia to be friends. Mia doesn't want dragging down. She has a bright future ahead of her.'

Click.

'Snooty cow,' I said to myself. Besides, Mia wasn't a child. She was quite capable of deciding who to be friends with. I'd send Mia an e-mail as soon as I could. I picked up the phone again and dialled home. It was a relief when Marcus answered.

'Hey there, Squirt!' I said.

'Jenna!' He sounded pleased to hear my voice. 'Mum's out getting a few things for our surprise holiday to Florida.'

I cheered up. I wasn't being exiled to Sarah's for the summer after all! Mum had been winding me up. I suppose I deserved it for giving her such a hard time. Yippee! Sun, sand and roller-coasters!

'When do we leave?' I asked.

'We're getting the plane tonight. We've got a house in Florida for three weeks,' Marcus continued excitedly.

'What about me? Are you picking me up on the way, or shall I get a train?' I asked as Marcus rattled on, oblivious.

'A friend of Mum's had two spare places available at the last minute. Mum says we deserve a break after all the stress you've put this family through. She was going to tell you tonight.'

'Sarah's phone has been cut off,' I said.

Mia had been to Florida and now I was desperate to go to the shopping malls and theme parks that she'd told me about. I couldn't believe that they were really going without me.

'I hope you both have a lovely time!' I said sarcastically.

'Thanks, Jenna,' he said. 'I'll send you a postcard.'

I stayed in the phone box for a long while, shocked by the news. Then all my emotions started sparking off like fireworks inside me. I stumbled across the road and followed a public footpath sign through a field. The path led to a stile and then into another field.

How could Mum even consider going away without me? The stress *I'd* put them through? What about me? Admittedly, I had been pushing things with her in the weeks before the last incident. Coming in late at night, spending a lot of my time at Mia's house, talking on the phone with Jackson and lying about having done all my schoolwork. But that was only the usual stuff that kids did to wind up their parents. Did she hate me so much that she wanted me grounded in a Netherby hell instead of flying in a roller-coaster heaven? It's not easy getting excluded from school. Did Mum stop for one minute to wonder how I was feeling? That what I might need right now was some support and encouragement, instead of being sent away from home? I certainly wouldn't be getting any here. Aunt Sarah was incapable of being in charge of a tin of soup, let alone a human being.

I sat down in the shade of a tree and looked round. With no one in sight, I unpacked that section of my mind that stored all my unhappy feelings about Mia and Jackson, and mixed them with how I felt about being abandoned by Mum and Marcus. Then all my anger, hurt and sadness bubbled up into a liquid that I let out as ugly great blobs of tears. I'd been bottling things up for too long – time I let it all out and had a really good cry.

A few minutes of this and I was feeling much better.

I was blowing my nose when a stick dropped from the tree above and landed at my feet, followed by a rustling sound. I looked up, expecting to see a bird or a squirrel, but to my surprise it was a girl. Her hair was tied in tight plaits and she was wearing a pair of homemade dungarees and an intense expression.

'Trees don't like crying. It upsets them,' she said as she

worked her way down a branch and landed at my feet. She patted the bark, sat down beside me and added, 'You're not from round here.'

She was about ten years old, but she spoke in a clipped voice, like a child actor in an old black-and-white film.

She kept on staring at me until I cracked under the pressure to say something. 'I'm Jenna and I'm working in the bookshop.'

The girl smiled. 'I'm Aurora. It means the dawn. I was called that because I arrived bright and early. Sarah's cool. She lent my brother a book about trees and we play this great game. He brings me a leaf and I have to guess what type of tree it comes from.'

'That sounds exciting,' I said brightly. A few more days in Netherby and I would probably be driven by boredom to playing that game.

'We'll come into the shop soon. My brother loves books.'

I stood up to go. 'Will you be all right here in the middle of nowhere by yourself?'

The girl burst out laughing. 'I live here, silly. That's my treehouse.' She pointed up to a wooden building, hidden amongst the branches, and said solemnly, '*All* these trees, flowers and fields belong to me. As far as your eyes can see and beyond, it's all mine.'

I smiled back, waiting for her to introduce me to her imaginary pixie friends who lived in the tree with her.

The girl smiled back at me. 'I like you, Jenna. You look strange.'

'Thanks a bunch,' I said.

'You don't look like anyone else around here. I like the way your hair is red and brown with yellow stripes in it.'

'They're highlights,' I said.

'They're wonderful,' she gasped.

I laughed. She was cute in a funny, tree-elfish sort of way.

'Your eyes are green like a cat's eyes. I bet you're interesting.' She stared up at me.

I laughed again. 'I'm not. My Mum will tell you what a pain I am. I never do what I'm told.'

Aurora shrieked with laughter, put on an even posher voice and waggled her finger at me. 'Are you wilful and have no regard for authority?'

I smiled. 'Definitely.'

'Were you crying because you were mad at someone?' she asked.

I nodded and said, 'I'm mostly mad at myself.'

'My mum gets mad at herself when she can't fit into her party dress. My brother gets really cross when he's not feeling well. Why are you mad?'

There was another rustling noise in the tree. I looked up, half expecting to see a pixie, but there was nothing there. 'Everything and anything can drive me nuts!' I said. 'From the way my hair sticks up in the morning to the way we're treating the planet. Worst of all, I hate the fact that if I have two choices, I always end up making the wrong one.'

There was another rustling sound from the tree.

'Is there anyone else up there?' I asked, suddenly feeling panicked. Was there another witness to my crying fest? As if on cue, there was a tiny meow.

Aurora giggled. 'It's only Curiosity, my cat. We call him Curio for short. You can be a friend of mine, Jenna.'

I bowed my head and grinned. 'Thank you. I am deeply honoured. Goodbye.'

Aurora giggled again. 'See you again soon, Jenna. I like you.'

Even though she was obviously not from this planet, I liked her too.

The Mini-Mart was surprisingly well stocked. It even had three types of cat food to choose from.

'Tallulah likes Gourmet Puss,' the woman behind the counter said. The fact that everyone seemed to know me was freaking me out. In London I have neighbours who have lived next door since I was a baby and still wouldn't be able to pick me out in a police line-up, let alone identify my cat's favourite food.

'What does Curio like to eat, then?'

The woman frowned at me. It was good to know that they didn't know absolutely everything about everyone. Then again, tree elves probably couldn't afford to buy cat food.

When I got back, Sarah had got dressed and was sitting out in the garden with a large pot of tea.

She sighed. 'I'm feeling a bit better.'

I told her about my encounters with Julius and Ava in the shop, but I didn't mention Aurora. I liked to keep my crying fests as private as possible.

Sarah poured some tea. 'I should've warned you about them. But they're both harmless.'

'What about the Rampant Romantics? How harmless are they?'

'Be afraid. Be very afraid . . . The Rampant Romantics take their quest for a good love story very seriously,' Sarah said, grinning. 'They have an insatiable appetite for romance.'

I mimed sticking a finger down my throat to gag myself, then asked, 'How many of them are there?'

'Only three hardcore members. Ava is the most prolific romance reader. She has been known to read four books in one day. Then there's Gina and Muriel. They run the charity shop.'

I sniffed. 'I can't think of anything more boring than constantly reading soppy love stories.'

'That's because you haven't been in love yet . . .' Sarah started and then stopped herself and frowned. 'I'm sorry. That was so patronising of me. You've probably been in love dozens of times.'

To draw the heat away from my so-called love life, I asked, 'How many times have you been in love, then?'

Now it was Sarah's turn to fluff around. 'That's a difficult one . . .'

I instantly regretted the question. I wasn't ready to listen to any kind of answer that Sarah was going to give me. She wasn't fitted with 'child filters' the way Mum was. Mum would have told me to butt out or given just as much information as I could cope with. Sarah was unpredictable.

'I've had lovers . . .' Sarah began.

I cringed. *Please, please don't go into detail about your love life . . .*

'And there have been times when I *thought* it was love, but I think my answer would have to be twice. I have been in love on two occasions in my life.'

Then, before I could stop myself, I asked, 'What's the difference between *thinking* it's love and knowing that you are in love? That it's not just a stupid crush or something.' I was thinking of how mixed-up I felt about Jackson.

'You know it's love because you would risk anything for the person. Even the awful pain of their leaving.' Sarah's face started to crumple, but instead of breaking down she stood up, looked at her watch and said, 'It's a quarter past five now. You can stay here and relax. I'll go back and run the shop for a couple of hours. We get a few tourists staying in Netherby at this time of year.'

'Will you be wanting me to work there again?' I asked.

'I'm counting on your help, Jenna. The summer is a busy time for the shop. I'll pay you when I can. See you later.'

I went back up to my bedroom, lay down on the bed and took out the crumpled photo of Jackson for the first time since leaving London. That boy was cute even when he was doing his best to look mean and moody. He was much more classically teen-mag model good-looking than Torso Boy.

I smiled as I remembered the day Jackson had given me the photo. It was one of those rare times when there was just the two of us. Mia had been off school with a bad cold. Jackson had to go and renew his bus pass and afterwards we decided to catch the bus into Leicester Square and grab a slice of pizza. We spent ages hanging around the square watching the different types of people come and go.

We played this stupid game called 'That's Your Boyfriend/ Girlfriend', which involved spotting a passer-by and quickly shouting out, 'That's your girlfriend!' The first person to shout it out won that round. The idea of the game, if there really was one, was to pick the highest number of outlandish people for your opponent and to shout it out the fastest. We played it for ages, laughing hysterically.

'You're cool, Jenna,' Jackson had said on the way back, as he handed me one of his photographs. When Mia saw them the next day she had insisted that we all cram into a photo booth and pose for more photos. That was fun too.

Mia was great company, but we were always ending up doing what she wanted. It had all started when she came to Coot's Hill in Year Eight when we were twelve years old. She knew how to handle the other girls and the teachers so that no one dared to get in her way. I was struggling with everything from making friends to keeping up with my coursework.

An image of Mia flashed into my brain. She was taller and skinnier than me. She was one and a half centimetres taller, to be precise. Her hair was longer, Dad richer than mine . . . Mia was keen on statistics, especially when they came out in her favour. There were never any limits on what Mia thought she could do. Mrs Andrews described her as a 'high achiever', but my Mum said 'attention seeking'. Mum never really got on with Mia, which is one reason I did.

Then Jackson transferred to the school last term. At primary school he had always been one of those annoying boys, obsessed with football cards and spouting Premier League scores. The most complicated thing he had ever said to me was, 'What team do you support?' He had gone on to a different secondary school and I hadn't thought about him for ages.

He'd undergone a growth spurt and transformed from a faceless geek to definite boyfriend material. Tall, muscular, well dressed. He didn't stand a chance. Mia was the tracer bullet and he was the target. When he started tagging along with us things got complicated. I knew that Mia liked him, but I wanted to spend some time alone with him too. I wanted him to kiss me. I wanted people to think that I was going out with him. I wanted it to be serious.

To try and shake off these thoughts of my past, I spent a long time washing my hair. Then I went out to sit in the back garden to let it dry and read a trashy crime novel that I'd found lying around in the living room. I was just getting absorbed in it when a brown beanie hat popped up from next-door's garden and said, 'Hi!'

For a split second I thought it might be Torso Boy, but when I looked up it was a tall, gangly lad of about seventeen. He smiled and said 'Hi' again.

I smiled back and said, 'Hi.'

'Great job on the garden. We heard you thrashing about in weed city earlier on,' he said, grinning. 'I'm Charlie.'

There was a sound of a door creaking open and another figure popped up from behind the fence. A taller, even ganglier version of Charlie, except he was wearing a thick silver chain round his neck.

'Who you scoping, bro?' he said in a distorted gangster-rap accent.

Charlie rolled his eyes, 'Meet Freddie, my kid brother.'

'Cool. Eye-candy,' he said, winking at me.

I glared back at him. He blushed and fiddled with the silver chain before disappearing back down the garden.

'Ignore him. It's just a phase he's going through. Last year it was cricket statistics, now it's hip-hop slang. There is no logic either – we play in an anti-folk band together.'

I nodded. 'Sarah told me about you two.'

'You should come to the village hall and hear us play sometime,' he said.

I nodded again. I seemed to have lost the power to construct sentences, which is really weird because when I'm with Mia and Jackson I never stop talking. It must be all this fresh country air affecting my brain, I thought.

Life was certainly taking on some strange twists and turns.

Maybe I could hang round with Charlie and Freddie for a while. I could even get to know Torso Boy. That wouldn't be so bad. At least until Mia got round to fessing up – then my life could go back to some kind of normality.

Chapter Six

After Charlie and Freddie had gone back inside I lay down on a smooth patch of grass in the garden and closed my eyes. The late afternoon sun was warm on my face and I told myself I was absorbing vitamin D and tried not to think about skin cancer or ageing. Mia was big on ageing skin. She never left the house without smothering herself in SPF 25 sunscreen and lip protector.

It was Mia who decided who we weren't going to like any more, or who was going to have a trick played on them. She decided which teachers we needed to impress and whose life was going to be made a misery. She was the one who told me to leave the choir last term, as it was too uncool. That was tough, as I loved singing, but I was happy to go along with it. When you've known someone like Mia for a long time you become loyal and Mia's cool barometer was always spot on. Being known as one of Mia's friends made my life a lot easier at school.

Mia always felt that she had an automatic right to anything she wanted, whilst I always believed that I wasn't quite good enough. That was the big difference between us. Most of the time it was fun watching Mia take all the risks. I am the sort of a person that does 'being in the background' best. Mia had even said to me once, 'When I'm famous, you can be my personal assistant.'

Things didn't go according to plan for her with Jackson.

The more Mia tried to impress him the worse it got. She kept on asking Jackson for Jamaican slang words until he said, 'Why are you asking me? My mum is from Nigeria and my dad is from East London.'

Then there was the end-of-term disco. I was thrilled because Jackson grabbed me for the last dance and kissed me. He'd walked me home and said, 'See you around.'

Where was he now? Spending the summer in football training and being chased by girls. At least I never chased after him. He had asked *me* to dance. I was the one who he kissed at the end of the school disco.

If only I'd known then how momentous the events of that night would be I'd never have gone to the disco. There were too many repercussions . . .

My face was burning and I wasn't sure if it was from the sun or the force of that memory.

Chapter Seven

'We'll close the shop early and go over to the summer fête at Netherby Hall,' Sarah announced. 'It starts at two o'clock.'

'Whoopdeedoo,' I muttered under my breath. But at least it would be a change of scene.

It had been a tough week. There were hardly any browsers, let alone paying customers. One day the only visitor I had apart from Julius was Tallulah. She was only interested in washing herself in embarrassing places and snoozing on the velvet cushion.

It's amazing how motivating being bored out of your skull can be. The counter was polished to within an inch of its life. I also made sure that I was looking sophisticated at all times, keeping a half-opened Penguin Classic on the counter. I'd also discovered a dusty poetry book called *Vintage Verse*, and I was actually enjoying puzzling over lines of poetry. That's how bad it had got on the boredom front. Typical that when I was looking gorgeous and ready for him, Torso Boy was nowhere to be seen.

But this particular Saturday morning went by quickly, as there were actually some customers. When she was helping them, Sarah became a different person. She seemed more confident. She knew a lot about old books too. Mrs

MacLean from the chemist's was in seventh heaven because Sarah had tracked down an out-of-print book for her.

The only thing she wasn't good at was remembering to eat. So at about half past twelve I said, 'Think I'll go over to the café for a quick lunch break.'

The café was light and airy and I ordered a coffee and some internet time. The waitress had a trendy haircut and was unfriendly enough to work in London. I started to smile, then stopped and scowled back at her. Her coldness was a relief. It can be exhausting smiling and acknowledging everyone. Besides, I wanted some time to myself.

I sent Mum an e-mail telling her that I was fine and that Sarah was hoping to get the phone reconnected soon. I hoped she was having a fantastic holiday and said not to worry about me as I was being kept busy working in the shop and cooking and cleaning for Sarah. That should get some guilt money into the pot.

I spent a long time composing Mia's e-mail. I told her that I was sharing a cottage with and working for my aunt Sarah, who treated me like an adult. That Netherby was a funky place with its own summer festival. I also hinted that there was a mystery boy I was interested in. I said I hoped that her mum was not putting her under too much pressure over the schoolwork and that her dad would hurry up and return from his business trip so that she could get on with owning up to her part in what we had done.

Charlie and Freddie came into the café just as I was finishing my e-mail to Mia. They were wearing matching beanie hats and Freddie was wearing a hideous pair of tinted sunshades. When he saw me he raised his fist and said, 'It's Jenna, my homegirl,' then sprawled himself out on the chair next to me and puffed himself into a mean pose. When he saw that Charlie had bought himself a cake he whined, 'Didn't you get me a cake? That's not fair!'

Charlie grinned at me and asked pointedly, 'Would you like something to eat, Jenna?'

I shook my head.

Freddie said, 'How about another coffee, innit? I'll order you one.' He sprang out of his seat and swaggered to the counter.

'How long will this hip-hop slang phase last?' I asked Charlie.

'Too long,' Charlie said, laughing. 'The worst thing is that because he's taller than me, people assume he's the oldest. But I'm the one who's seventeen and he's two years younger than me.'

'That must be tough. Marcus, my brother, is only eight so I don't have that problem,' I said.

'He drives me crazy sometimes,' he said, 'and sometimes he just makes me laugh. He is a great guitarist, though. He stays in his room practising for hours and hours, which is great for the band. What's not so great is having to ring Mum every night to let her know he's OK.'

The Ice Maiden brought my coffee over. She had slopped the coffee into the saucer.

'Hi Cleo, have you met Jenna?' Charlie said.

She nodded and opened her lips just wide enough to let out a strained hello.

'She's staying at Sarah's,' Freddie explained whilst stuffing a large bite of Charlie's cake in his mouth.

'I'm working at the bookshop,' I added. For some reason, part of me wanted to impress her.

Cleo looked at me like I just announced I was a cleaner in the local sewage works and said, 'I never buy second-hand books.'

'I got a great cricket book there . . .' Freddie began, then he checked himself and reverted to his 'gansta mode'. 'Second-hand books aren't bling-bling enough!'

'I like working there!' I snapped back at both of them and angrily slurped my coffee.

Just then, another voice joined in. 'Second-hand bookshops are amazing places. You never know what you might find in them.'

My mind flashed back to the sight of his naked chest and I choked on my coffee. Charlie made matters worse by very helpfully thumping on my back.

At the sight of Torso Boy, Cleo transformed from Ice Maiden to Red-Hot Babe. Her eyes lit up and she gave him a long, touchy-feely, sick-making hug. She whispered something in his ear and was all over him like a rash. He didn't seem to be complaining either. Cleo whisked him off to show him something 'really important' at the other end of the café, leaving me to watch him from a distance.

I sipped my coffee and pretended to stare in the middle distance as my brain focused on Torso Boy. He was about my height, with a compact build and black hair that was in need of a cut. His T-shirt was too tight and his trainers were battered. His nose was long and poked out in a funny way. His mouth seemed too big for his face. He twitched a lot when he was talking.

The total effect was devastating.

Chapter Eight

I t wasn't just the heat that unsettled me as Sarah and I trudged up to Netherby Hall that afternoon. Images of Torso Boy kept jumping into my head, making me feel restless. Why had I even hinted to Mia about him? And hadn't I made up my mind not to bother about boys?

There was something different about Sarah. It took me ages to figure out what it was. Then it hit me – she wasn't jangling. I looked at her. She wasn't wearing her bracelets or her rings. I don't think I'd ever seen her without jewellery in my whole life.

She noticed me looking. 'Fancied a change of image, so I sold them. Look, there's Julius.'

She marched off before I could say anything.

Julius was busy 'organising' a group of boy scouts with buckets of water and sponges on the lawn.

He waved us over and said, 'You win a prize if you can hit me bang on the nose with a sponge. Great fun!' He pulled on a clown's nose.

'It's a picture of the Incredible Hulk with the face cut out,' one of the scouts piped up.

'Always fancied myself as a green muscle-bound monster,' Julius said, 'so I'm going to be the one who risks life and limb, or rather, life and noggin by poking my head through the hole.'

Julius stroked his whiskers with glee. A few of the scouts looked crestfallen. 'Tell you what,' he added, 'we'll take turns at poking our heads through. An old man like me can only take so many soakings.'

That seemed to cheer them up a bit. They reminded me of Marcus. My brother loved any excuse to get soaked. I felt a pang. Never in a thousand years did I ever think that I could miss my eight-year-old brother! All I really ever cared about was hanging out with my friends. I could tell you how Mia was feeling every second of the day because we were always together. Jackson's thoughts were harder to fathom, but it was always fun trying to work him out.

I didn't have a single friend here, but I didn't care. I wasn't going to be around for much longer and no friends meant that there was no one to hurt you.

The lawn was getting crowded. I took a closer look at Netherby Hall. It was a huge mansion house, built in a crumbling pink stone. There were two large bay windows at the front and a huge front door. The vast front lawn was filled with stalls and had a brass band in one corner. Someone had lit a barbecue and small curls of white smoke and a smell of fried onions filled the air.

I felt a claw-like grip on my arm.

'Hello, Ava,' I said.

She prodded me and nudged me towards the house. 'Hurry up. I've saved you a place. You can pay me later.'

I didn't have a clue what she was talking about. I frowned. 'I'm not having my face painted.'

'What are you going on about? We're going on a tour of

the house. Hugh Netherby opens it only once a year. It's a real bun-struggle to get a place, so come on.'

I didn't have the heart to tell her that I couldn't care less what the inside of Netherby Hall looked like.

Ava began chatting to the two ladies from the charity shop. She introduced them as Muriel and Gina from the Rampant Romantics. It was hard to tell who was who because they had identical hairstyles.

I made a mental note never to go to Ava's for a haircut, then asked, 'Who are the Netherbys?' I'd never got round to asking Julius.

Ava explained. 'The Netherby family has lived on the site for centuries. They own most of the land round here, which is why everything is called after them. There was a wobble in the nineteenth century following the tragic early death of Eveline. The estate passed on to some distant cousin who'd been working as a poor clerk in London.'

'Eveline was a famous beauty, but she died before she could marry and provide a son and heir. Struck down by consumption, she was. Just faded away,' Muriel added, shaking her head sadly.

'I can never understand why women couldn't inherit,' I said, as we walked into the main entrance hall.

'We are the weaker sex, don't you know!' Muriel said, and they all giggled.

Ava nudged me and whispered, 'That's why both their husbands died years ago and we're still tough as old boots.' She ran her finger across a piece of furniture and tutted.

Gina nodded in agreement. 'Needs a good clean.'

The entrance hall had a dusty, shabby look, but it was still pretty amazing. The walls were covered in a dark wood panelling and the flagstone floor was covered with faded Turkish rugs.

Our tour guide, Sheila, arrived. We were allowed to see the private garden, salon, dining room and a long gallery. After a while, I got fed up of being herded around, so I left the 'gals' clucking over a hideous china tea set and sneaked back to take a closer look at the gallery.

Although the room was deserted it didn't feel empty. It had absorbed so much life over the centuries that it was filled with atmosphere. The sunlight shone through the windows, causing the specks of dust to flicker and dance in its beams. My footsteps creaked on the floorboards as I walked down the long gallery.

I stopped at the portrait of Eveline Netherby. She was dressed up in a fantastic ball-gown and jewels, but there was no aristocratic smugness about her. One of her hands lightly grasped a fan that looked as if it was about to fall. The fingers of her other hand gently touched a jewelled brooch that was pinned to her dress close to her heart. She was smiling, but her eyes ached with sadness.

A floorboard creaked. I assumed that it was Ava, come to get me.

'Do you think she knew she was going to die?' I said.

There was a pause, then a familiar voice – but not Ava's. 'We all die one day.'

'Not me!' I said jokingly as I turned round to see Torso Boy standing in a pool of sunlight, holding a bunch of beautiful white roses. For a moment, before he smiled at me, it seemed to me that his eyes had the same sadness as Eveline's. There was something unreal about his pose, like he was a portrait that had suddenly come to life.

The sight of him made everything inside me work in slow motion, except my heart, which went into fast-forward.

His laughter broke the spell as he came close and looked at the portrait. 'It's a great painting, but I prefer this one.'

He walked over to the other side of the room towards a portrait of a big fat man with laughing eyes and an equally round dog. Beside them was a large telescope.

'That's Septimus Netherby, a rogue who spent all his youth gambling and spending the family fortune. A bad attack of the gout turned his mind to gardening and star-gazing. He planted most of the trees around here and built the grotto and Greek temple in the garden. His best friend was Brutus, his dog. When Brutus died he built a huge mausoleum in the grounds. It's twice as large as the one he had built for his wife. His telescope is still in the library.'

'You know a lot,' I said, trying not to look at him.

'I spend a lot of time here.'

'I'd better go and catch up with Ava,' I said, but I didn't move. It was like he was a magnet and I was a lump of metal.

There was an awkward silence. He looked down at the roses and said, 'I'd better do something with these.'

We both turned away at the same time. He put the flowers in a large Chinese vase and we left the gallery by separate exits.

At least I wasn't wearing a cobweb headdress or spluttering this time.

I caught up with Ava and the gals in the gardens behind the house. Sheila, our tour guide, was explaining in great detail about the grotto and the temple and how they were called follies. I wasn't really listening and neither were Ava and the gals. They were swanning round the small Greek-style temple, pretending they were in a costume drama.

'Oh, Mr Darcy,' Ava said with a sigh, and wrung her hands. The others giggled.

A few people gave them dirty looks and Sheila went 'SSH!', but they just ignored them and carried on.

I wandered back to the front of the house and around the stalls for a while. There was a cosy, warm atmosphere, as everyone seemed to know each other. If Mia had been here we would have formed a tight unit and I'd probably be laughing now at how boring and childish it all was. Mia always hated events like this.

Someone tugged at my sleeve. 'Jenna, you have to have a go on my stall,' said Aurora, looking desperate. 'Everyone else is chicken.'

'Well, I'm not,' I said.

'You have to try and eat one of my special doughnuts in eight seconds.' She held up a large sugar-coated ring doughnut.

'Easy,' I said. I was feeling a bit hungry anyway.

'Without licking your lips,' Aurora added. 'If you do it, you win a pound.'

'Easy . . .' I said, a bit less convincingly this time. Fortunately, Aurora's stall was in a quiet corner and there weren't many people about.

As I began to bite into the largest, sugariest doughnut I'd ever seen, a group of scouts appeared and Aurora led them in a loud chorus of, 'Go Jenna, go Jenna!'

After the first bite, I was totally focused on winning. The sugar built up on my lips. The shrieking grew louder. Aurora had a stopwatch. My lips began to tingle and itch. I was desperate to lick them, but I held on. I could feel my tongue involuntarily slipping out. I bit down on it along with the doughnut. Victory was in sight when I caught a glimpse of two pairs of eyes looking at me. One was Cleo's. Her expression was a mixture of sneering and triumph. And next to her, grinning for all he was worth, was Torso Boy.

With only three seconds to go, I licked my lips and walked away as quickly as I could. What was it with me? Why did I always manage to make a fool of myself? I ran behind a marquee and rubbed at my lips. There was a metallic taste of blood in my mouth. I must've bitten down so hard on my tongue that I cut it. I was going to wait a few minutes and then go and find Sarah and tell her I was leaving.

'I thought you'd like this? It'll take away the sugary taste.'

It was him again!

Torso Boy held out a paper cup of water in front of me. Probably just coming along to have a laugh at me.

'Thanks,' I said coldly and took a sip from the cup.

He didn't take the hint; instead he sat down beside me.

'You were great. My best time is thirty seconds and Cleo is rubbish. She could only manage five seconds before licking.' He smiled at me.

He was so close to me that I could feel his arm next to mine, even though we weren't touching. He smelled earthy with a hint of lemon. I felt overpowered by the sense of him, and my brain emptied of anything interesting to say.

He just sat with me for a while. He had gentleness about him that I didn't know how to deal with. He wasn't like any of the boys I was used to. If it had been Jackson, he'd have been laughing the loudest at me. Then he would've tried to out-do me in the doughnut eating. Or he would've deliberately misunderstood the rules of the game and started a row or something. Both he and Mia would do anything to be the centre of attention. And I would've laughed along and joined in, burying my embarrassment in the noise.

This boy was different.

I could still taste the blood from my tongue.

'I'm bleeding,' I said.

He winced. 'Blood freaks me out,' he said and moved quickly away from me.

I stood up to leave.

'I'm sorry. I didn't mean to be rude,' he stammered.

'I have to go now,' I said, turning away.

'I could show you round later when everyone's gone.'

But I carried on walking away, whilst my brain was screaming, 'Fool! Fool! Fool!'

Chapter Nine

'**I**'m going away for a day or so on a book-buying trip. Julius will help you out in the shop and Ava will come round in the evenings,' Sarah announced on Monday morning.

Mum never trusted me to babysit for Marcus for more than a couple of hours. If she had to go out then she phoned every five minutes to check up. Here was Sarah proposing to go off for days and she was leaving me without a phone. I was shocked.

She wasn't totally irresponsible. She did leave me the address for the vet in case anything should happen to Tallulah. She also left me some food in the fridge, so I suppose I should have been grateful for that.

Julius was quite perky when I got to the shop. 'So good to be back at the helm once more,' he said before sinking back into his chair, stroking his whiskers and reading his book like he always did.

'Do second-hand bookshops ever make any money?' I asked him.

'A fortune can be made if you find the right book. Hope springs eternal.'

'What about old records?' I nudged Kai's box of records with my foot.

Julius nodded. 'The same rule applies. If it is rare and sought after and in good condition.' He handed me a couple of specialised antiquarian book magazines. 'Read them and weep.'

The television deprivation must be getting to me because I was actually interested. The amount of money some dusty old books fetched was amazing.

I was daydreaming about discovering a rare book when Aurora came in.

'No doughnuts, please.' I raised my hands in mock horror.

She giggled and tugged at her plaits. 'I've come to see you!' she said. 'Now that school has finished I'll come in lots. My brother's coming too. He goes to college in London but he's here for a while. He'll most probably buy a book. He usually does.'

Aurora chatted on and on at me about the stall and how much money she'd made, how many doughnuts she'd had to eat to test out the experiment, and how she was going to have a stall at the Netherby Festival. On and on she went without stopping to draw breath. I was glazing over. Then she announced in her clipped voice, 'You're coming to tea tomorrow.'

'Will there be room for me in your treehouse? Will Curio mind sharing?'

Aurora giggled. 'Oh, no! Mum is going to make a wild mushroom quiche. I'll meet you by my treehouse at three o'clock.'

The thought of dining in a treehouse with Aurora wasn't a wildly exciting prospect, but the chance of getting a proper meal was. Plus, I'd save some of the food money Sarah had left me.

'It's a deal,' I said, grinning. 'Julius won't mind watching the shop.'

The shop bell rang, Aurora frowned and said, 'Gabriel, what took you so long? I've invited Jenna to come to tea.'

'She's nagged you to death, then,' he said, grinning at me.

So his name was Gabriel!

Still grinning, he added, 'She's not very good at taking no for an answer.' He leaned on the counter and looked at my magazine and asked, 'You interested in books, then?'

I paused, trying to think of an answer. But he answered for me.

'Silly question when you're working here.'

'I'm helping Sarah out,' I said. Why had my voice gone all soft and quiet?

Aurora jumped up on the counter between us. 'Ssh, you'll wake Julius. When is he going to finish that book?'

Julius had nodded off with the book balanced expertly on his lap.

'He's been reading it for years,' Gabriel said with a laugh. His accent was a bit posh, like Aurora's. Then he glanced over my shoulder at the box of records. 'Kai still not back, then?'

'Not for the foreseeable future,' I muttered.

'He will be. He wouldn't take off for ever and leave his precious record collection behind. Can I just have a look?'

He jumped over the counter and headed for the cardboard box. I suppose living in trees made him agile. He crouched down and began flicking through the collection.

'What's Kai like?' I asked. I was interested to know what he thought.

Aurora butted in. 'Mum says he's a free spirit with a deep poetic soul.'

Gabriel tugged on one of her plaits and frowned. 'She did not!'

'Did too! I heard her talking about him. She said he needed to be free from that millstone.'

I felt a pang. How could anyone describe Sarah as a millstone? You'd have to be pretty lightweight yourself if you thought she was a millstone.

Gabriel nudged Aurora and looked at me as he said, 'Jenna doesn't want to hear your prattle, Aurora. Kai's all right. Sometimes he lends me some of his records. I play in a band and he helps out with the sound checking.'

He said my name like he'd known me for ever.

Chapter Ten

That evening, Ava came round with a fantastic meaty stew. As I stuffed myself Ava settled herself in on the sofa with a large cardboard box.

'I'm making pom-poms for the Brownies,' she announced as she took out some pieces of cardboard and began winding wool around them.

As I was finishing my second bowlful she said, 'I hear you're a troubled teen.'

I snorted. 'Don't spare my feelings.'

Ava carried on, 'I'm quite good with troubled teens, and babies going through the terrible twos. They're quite similar really. Lots of screaming and face pulling.'

'And you are such an expert on troubled teens because . . . ?' I arched an eyebrow at her the way Mia always did at supply teachers.

Ava took another sip of her frothy coffee and blinked. 'On account of having been one myself.'

'Don't tell me, you stayed up till midnight and didn't wear your slippers!' I laughed.

'Is that your idea of wildness? What I did was dance naked in the grounds of Netherby Hall, fall in love with the wrong boy and make lots of foolish mistakes.'

I looked away at the thought of a naked Ava. As if on cue Tallulah began to mew loudly. I leaped off my chair and dashed into the kitchen to feed her and to have a quiet laugh at the thought of a 'wild' Ava. I composed myself and went back in the lounge.

'Being a beautiful woman can be a terrible burden,' Ava continued as she reached into a handbag and pulled out some extra-strong mints and some tatty old photographs.

The first photo was a small black-and-white one of a pretty, dark-haired girl with a familiar grin.

'If I knew then what I know now . . .' Ava's voice quivered.

'What does that mean?' I asked. Grumbling older people always said that.

Ava laughed. 'You're right. It is a silly thing to say. It would mean transplanting my old brain into my young body.'

'Yuck! Sounds like a plot for a bad science fiction movie,' I said.

'All the mistakes I've made and life experiences I've had have created the person I am now. If I hadn't let my young self do all those daft and crazy things where would I be now?'

'So it's OK to be crazy when you're young?' I asked.

'It's all part of growing up. Then you have to be respectable for about thirty years before you get to be reckless all over again!' Ava laughed.

I casually flicked through the rest of the photographs.

Ava's voice went quiet. 'Some mistakes can be more painful than others. It would be nice to unmake one or two of those painful ones. Mistakes should be like reverse wishes. You should be able to unmake three mistakes in your life.'

I stared at a photograph of a young woman standing in the grounds of Netherby Hall. She wasn't looking at the camera or smiling. It must have been a cold, windy day because her long, blond hair was blowing about and she was wearing a brown suede jacket. 'She's beautiful,' I said, sighing.

Ava looked at the photo and sighed too. 'Lavinya had an effortless beauty. Never wore make-up or did her hair, but she always looked just right. Broke his heart, she did. One day she was here and the next she had gone. No one knew where or why. She was a wild spirit. You couldn't pin her down. I found that picture in an old book in Sarah's shop. Someone must've been using it as a bookmark and forgotten about it. She'd be in her mid-twenties there. She died a few years ago. No one speaks about her now. Especially not the second Lady Netherby.'

'Lavinya was the first Lady Netherby?' I asked.

'Yes, and Gabriel is her son. Aurora is the child from Lord Netherby's second marriage or it might even be his third. There have been a succession of girlfriends and wives at Netherby Hall over the years and I find it hard to keep track.' Ava carried on winding the wool.

'Gabriel and Aurora live at Netherby Hall!' I gasped. And here was me imagining that they lived in a caravan in the countryside – or in a tree!

'Aurora's always lived there and Gabriel visits from time to time. Lord Netherby only found out he had a son when Gabriel was about eleven years old. He's a nice lad, even if he didn't inherit Lavinya's striking blond looks.'

'Aurora's invited me round for tea tomorrow,' I said. Gabriel's looks seemed just fine to me.

'That'll be nice, dear, but you should really be mixing with people of your own age. Why don't you pop into the youth club in the village hall? It's on every Monday night. You could call in for an hour or so. I won't mind.'

I muttered a vague reply. I didn't take in what she was saying. I was too busy trying to get my head round the fact that Torso Boy was Gabriel, son of Lord Netherby.

I'd seen TV programmes about the aristocracy and seen pictures galore of toffs in magazines, but Gabriel was nothing like them. He was so scruffy for one thing . . . I suppose if you have heaps of money you don't need to think so much about your appearance. Then another thought hit me.

What do you wear when you go to tea with a lord?

Ava made another milky coffee, but before she could drink it she'd dozed off on the sofa, making little snorting sounds. When her face was relaxed with sleep she looked a lot younger. I made a mental note to actually listen to her more.

The sound of a key turning in the lock startled me. I didn't expect Sarah for another day at least, but you never knew with her.

'We're in here!' I shouted.

'And who are *you*, exactly?' a man's voice replied.

Chapter Eleven

He looked me up and down and whistled.

'Jenna, you've grown up all of sudden.'

Shame you haven't, I thought.

'Sarah not here, then?' Something in his voice made me think that he knew she wouldn't be. He was carrying a large canvas bag.

Ava woke up with a start, 'Kai, love, you're back! Sarah will be pleased.'

'I only stopped by to pick up a few bits and pieces. Then we're off to a festival in Cornwall,' he said as he bent over and kissed Ava on the cheek.

I'd bet anything the other part of 'we' was young and female.

'Sarah didn't say you'd be coming round,' I said.

Kai grinned back at me and asked, 'Where is she?'

'She's gone on a book-buying trip,' Ava replied.

'She probably forgot to mention I was coming.'

Hadn't Sarah gone on and on about how she hadn't heard from him? Surely Ava would see through him.

'Ava, you're looking lovely as usual. Is that a new hair colour?' He tickled her cheek. Ava turned to mush.

I tried another tactic. 'I'll give you a hand, Kai.'

'No need, unless you'd like to rummage in my underwear drawer.'

He was holding a pretty big bag for just underwear.

'Wouldn't have thought you'd wear any,' I said. Now it was his turn to blush a bit. He came up close and cupped my face in his hand.

'Quite the sassy lady, aren't you?' he said and our eyes locked.

A horn sounded outside. Kai went to the window and waved. I could just make out the hunched figure of a young girl at the steering wheel, looking worried.

'I'd love to stay and get to know you better, but I'm in a bit of a hurry.' He left the room.

The upstairs floorboards creaked as he walked around opening and closing drawers and cupboards. I met him at the front door.

'Any message for Sarah?' I asked as he was on his way out.

'Sarah and I don't need formal conventions to communicate, but tell her I'll be back for the Netherby Festival.' As he was leaving, he leaned forward to kiss me on the cheek.

I left Ava to her photos and went out into the garden for some gulps of fresh air. It was a warm, light evening. I'd been away from home for nearly three weeks. I stretched out my arms and spun round in a great big circle. The air was hot and filled with tight gangs of insects. I felt a little crazed, affected by the mixture of emotions that swirled around inside me.

There was something about Kai that made my flesh creep. And there was something about Gabriel that made me feel awkward and unsure of myself.

What was it about Gabriel? He wasn't the best-looking lad I'd ever seen. Jackson was more handsome than he was.

Whenever I met Gabriel it was like an allergic reaction. I was itchy and uncomfortable in my body. Feeling like this was way too much to handle on top of waiting for Mia to speak out.

As it was only half past eight and I couldn't face an evening in the house with just Ava and the effect of Kai's visit eating away at me, I decided to go and check out the youth club.

'Take the box of pom-poms, will you?' Ava pushed the box at me. 'Now, I'll just see if Charlie or Freddie is around. He can escort you there.' She marched out into the back garden and yelled 'Yoohoo!' over the fence.

So, not only did I have to walk into a roomful of strangers carrying a box of pom-poms but I had to have an escort. Lucky for me Freddie was out, so it was Charlie who came to the door.

'See that you bring Jenna home at a reasonable time,' Ava called out as we set off down the lane. Charlie grinned.

'I don't know who she thinks she is ordering people around like that. Pay no attention to her,' I said, bristling.

Charlie shrugged his shoulders. 'Ava's all right. Just don't let her anywhere near your hair. Everyone who goes in that shop comes out with the same bouffant hairdo.'

I laughed. 'I know – I've seen Muriel and Gina.'

'You were lucky to catch me. I should've left twenty minutes ago. Our band is playing at the youth club tonight.'

'Anti-folk music, right?' I said, trying to sound smarter than I felt.

'What kind of music do you like, Jenna?' Charlie asked.

It was one of those trick questions that boys are always asking. Fortunately I had an answer ready.

'I have an eclectic taste in music,' I said.

Charlie wasn't for giving up. 'OK, name the last CD that you bought.'

'Howling Wolf,' I replied. I'd bought it for my grandad's birthday.

Charlie stopped dead in his tracks and nodded. 'That's cool,' he said.

We'd just reached the front of the village hall. It was a red-brick building with mock Tudor black-and-white-painted beams on the front. The date 1902 was carved above the door-way and a group of kids were hanging around by the entrance.

'What's your band called?' I asked as a battered white van pulled up beside us.

'Goats in a Spin,' Charlie replied as the back door of the van opened and my Number-One Fan, Cleo, jumped out and scowled at me. The door to the driver's seat opened, coming between me and Cleo, and a pair of faded jeans and battered trainers came out. They were Gabriel's.

'Hi, Gabe,' Charlie said. 'You know Jenna.'

He looked at me and smiled for a split second, then his expression changed and he said, 'Come on, Charlie, we've got fifteen minutes to set up.' It was like he couldn't be bothered wasting his time talking to me.

So his friends called him Gabe. Gabriel probably sounded too . . . angelic.

'Gabe plays the drums and Cleo sings a few songs from time to time,' Charlie explained. I put on my most bored expression.

Cleo came over and said, 'Still working in the bookshop for Soppy Sarah?'

'Sarah is my aunt,' I said, hoping that would embarrass her.

'Worse luck,' she replied. 'Relatives always pay you peanuts.'

Gabe (as I now thought of him) deliberately bumped into

her with the amp he was carrying. 'Shut up, Cleo.' He didn't look at me.

She laughed like he'd said something incredibly amusing and flicked a speck of dust from his hair in the way that you can only do when you're really close to someone.

I shook the pom-pom box and said, 'I'd better go and deliver these.'

'I'll give you a hand.' Charlie made a move for the box.

I pulled the other way. 'I can manage, Charlie.'

He went on ahead regardless and made a big fuss of opening the doors for me.

'Cleo is famous for her sharp tongue,' he told me. 'You get used to it after a while.'

I didn't bother to reply. Mia would've dealt with Cleo with a put-down or a look. My tactic was not to be impressed by any of them. Apart from Charlie, they didn't show any interest in me so why should I care about them and their poxy band? It wasn't as if they were friends of mine. And boys were off my radar at the moment.

I bought myself a packet of slightly out-of-date crisps from the vicar and sat down at the back of the hall as far away from where the band was setting up as I could get.

After a lot of faffing around with cables and endless sound checks they began to play. Charlie was the lead singer. Charlie and Freddie both played guitars whilst Gabe played drums. Cleo joined in with the others with the singing.

A gaggle of kids formed round the front. I stayed obstinately at the back and listened. Freddie had problems keeping time, but there was something edgy about them. The lyrics weren't bad either. They all took turns singing. Charlie had a soft, soulful singing voice.

I tried not to look at Gabe too much, but when I did he was playing with a frantic nervous energy. His chest tightened as he punched the beat with strained arms that seemed to move randomly. Sweat made his hair curl round his neck. His eyes were closed and he was totally absorbed in making music.

It took a couple of songs for my ears to adjust to their sound, but my body moved to the rhythm and my heart responded to the lyrics. Goats in a Spin were good. Part of me wanted to rush over and cheer, but another part felt awkward and shy and held me back.

At the end, Charlie came over and handed me a plastic cup of orange squash. I hate orange squash, but I didn't want to hurt his feelings so I took a sip and tried not to screw my face up.

'You don't like it? Shall I get you a can of Coke?' Charlie said, looking a little hurt by my reaction.

I took a deep breath and was about to say 'You were good' when Freddie came over.

'No, I bet the lady prefers Cristal.'

'And what is Cristal?' I asked him. My voice sounded harsher than I'd meant it to.

'Er . . . er, a very expensive drink,' Freddie floundered.

I floundered too as I started to say 'You were good' again, but before I could get the words out, another voice cut in.

'It's champagne,' Gabe explained. They probably drink it every day at his house!

Charlie turned to me and said, 'If you wait till we've packed up we can give you a lift home. We're getting some chips on the way back too.' I nodded gratefully at Charlie.

'We could pick up some doughnuts for you,' Gabe said and everybody laughed.

Cleo imitated Aurora's plummy voice, 'Go Jenna, go Jenna!'

Everybody laughed. My face felt scorched with embarrassment.

'No thanks. I've got to go home and do something . . . I've got to change the cat litter tray.'

I marched straight out of the door. I wasn't going to be laughed at for a moment longer.

Chapter Twelve

I t was like that old horror story about a man with two personalities, *Dr Jekyll and Mr Hyde*. One of them is nice and the other is a murderous monster. That how I felt at that moment. Only I didn't need to swallow any potion to change. All it took for my personality to wobble was to see Gabe.

What I really wanted now was a good chat with Mum. We used to talk for hours on end about anything and everything. I imagined her and Marcus screaming with joy on a rollercoaster. All Mum and I seemed to do now was have rows or not speak to each other at all. I was getting really good at that; keeping my feelings all bottled up until they exploded into tears.

I went straight upstairs, hurled myself on my pillow and sobbed my heart out. If you asked me to explain why, I wouldn't have been able to tell you. It had something to do with my feelings getting too big for my body again and a lot to do with being made to feel a fool in front of people.

What was it about me, anyway? I just didn't seem to be able to fit in anywhere. I was hopeless at school and Mia's friendship always made me feel inadequate like I was never quite good enough. I wanted to be able to stand up for myself but I didn't know what I wanted to make a stand about!

A light tapping noise at the window startled me. As I pulled back the curtain and squinted out of the window I had to duck the next stone that was flying towards the window.

A voice whispered, 'Have you finished changing the cat litter tray yet?'

'Yes,' I hissed back and as I leaned out of the window I smiled at my answer to Gabe's question, feeling like an absurd Juliet.

'Come for a walk with me. It's a beautiful evening. I'll wait for you at the front.' He leaped back over the wooden fence.

My first instinct had been not to go, but since when had my first instincts got me anywhere? So I splashed my face with cold water, pulled on my clothes, took a deep breath and went outside.

Gabe was sitting on an old stone wall opposite the house. There was a faint thud of music coming from Charlie's place. Gabe's legs twitched in time to the music.

We headed off down the lane in silence for a bit, then Gabe said, 'Sorry for the cheap doughnut jokes. I will never mention the "d" word again. Though, I have to say that I am truly impressed by your ability in that department.'

I noticed how soft and warm the tone of his voice was despite the well-rounded vowels.

'Sorry for my "changing the cat litter tray" put-down,' I replied.

Gabe laughed. 'That was funny – and so quick. I usually only think of things like that to say afterwards.'

'Me too, usually.'

It was a beautiful warm evening with a half-moon in the sky.

'Where I live it's never dark or quiet,' I said.

'I go to college there. Do you miss London?' Gabe asked as

he sat down under a tree. I stayed standing, but leaned against the trunk.

'I'm not sure if I miss it exactly. It's just the people there. They seem more real when you've left them behind. Or maybe it's just that you can understand your own feelings about them better from a distance.'

Gabe leaned back on the other side of the tree trunk.

'And what are your feelings about the people you've left behind?'

'Mixed. Sometimes I miss them but mostly I feel relieved to be away from them for a while. It gives me some space to think,' I said as I became aware of the tip of Gabe's elbow touching mine.

I moved my arm away slowly and stroked the bark.

'What is anti-folk music? I am sick of pretending that I have any idea what it is,' I said, laughing.

Gabe grinned. 'It's easier to tell you what it isn't. It's a reaction to manufactured pop music.'

I nodded. 'All those boy and girl bands and *Pop Idol* stuff. It is getting pretty boring.'

'That stuff is so phoney. They're told what to wear, how to sing in a certain way, what to say in interviews. Like they haven't got any opinions of their own. No one sings about anything that really matters.' He looked down at his watch and grabbed my arm. 'Come on, run! We can just make it.'

'No way am I . . .' I started to say before I was pulled along.

We raced down a hill, across a field and down through a graveyard. We stopped next to the churchyard. My lungs were bursting and my heart was banging on my chest to be let out.

Gabe put his arm around me as the bells from the church

tower began to ring out. We counted twelve muffled rings.

'Is there somebody in there?' I asked, still catching my breath.

'The vicar has to sit there all through the night and ring the bell.'

'You are kidding me!' I said. Then I looked at the expression on Gabe's face.

He laughed. 'Urban urchin.'

'Country bumpkin.'

'Mall rat.'

'Tree hugger.'

'Jenna hugger.' Gabe drew closer and hugged me tight. I could feel the warmth of his breath on my face. We didn't speak or move for a long time.

'Jenna.' His voice sounded serious.

'Gabe.' I echoed his tone.

He laughed. 'Let's do this again tomorrow night. But let's not tell anyone. It'll be like our time together. When the others are around, things get complicated. I'll meet you by the wall at nine.'

'I'll see if I can make it,' I said casually, knowing that whatever happened I would be there tomorrow night.

Gabe took hold of my hand and we walked back to Sarah's in silence.

'See you tomorrow,' he said when we got to the door.

Sarah came back early the next morning. After she had made a huge fuss of Tallulah, she turned to me. 'Sorry to leave you. I just needed to get away.'

'I thought you were buying some books.'

Sarah looked a bit sheepish. 'Oh yes, I did manage to pick up some. Were you all right?'

'Ava cooked me some great food. I went to the youth club and Aurora invited me for tea today . . . and Kai came back.'

Sarah's face flickered with hope, so I added quickly, 'To collect some of his stuff.'

'Did he leave a message?' Sarah said weakly.

'Just that he'll be back for the festival.' I tried to make my voice sound neutral, as if I didn't know how much the news would be hurting Sarah. No one likes to be pitied, do they?

Chapter Thirteen

I spent most of Tuesday trying to decide what to wear for tea with Aurora. I deliberately hadn't brought many clothes with me and Sarah's wardrobe wasn't worth raiding. By rights I should have been spending three weeks wearing a bikini and sunbathing on a Florida beach with Mum and Marcus.

Why hadn't I asked Gabe last night if he was going to be there? Part of me felt that I had dreamed our meeting last night. It had been too perfect. I tugged at my hair with a comb and tried on another T-shirt.

Sarah knocked lightly on my door. 'Can I come in?'

I nodded, but she hovered in the doorway.

'It's a bit awkward, Jenna,' she began. I put the comb down and swallowed hard. Maybe she wanted me to leave.

Sarah cleared her throat. 'I seem to have lost a vase that was in the bathroom. It belonged to your gran. And it's valuable. I was wondering if you'd broken it or something.'

It took me a while to think which vase she was talking about, there was so much clutter about the place. Then I remembered the garish orange-and-black-patterned monstrosity of a jug on the window ledge. Mum had one like it too, except in our house it was in a display case. Mum liked to show it off because it was by a woman called Clarice Cliff and it was worth a small fortune.

'Only it means a lot to me,' Sarah continued. Then it clicked. She was accusing me of taking it!

'Why don't you ask Kai about it?' I suggested as softly as I could. You didn't have to be Inspector Morse to work out that he'd be the most likely suspect.

Sarah sank down on the bed. 'What would he want with it? He knows how I've always loved that vase.'

I flared up. 'So you're blaming me instead.'

Sarah swallowed. 'I've heard that you'd been up to some pretty wild things. The school even considered calling the police.'

My head reeled. So this is what it was like when you got labelled. You get to go to the front of the blame queue. Part of me wanted to yell out loud something like, 'Oh, that vase! The one that I smashed into a thousand pieces and chucked through the window. If I'd known how much it meant to you I would have done it in front of you!'

Instead I stormed out of the room and raced down the stairs, sending Tallulah running for cover as I slammed the front door behind me.

It was starting to lightly rain as I made my way to the Mini-Mart so I sheltered in the phone box.

On impulse, I dialled Mia's number.

'It's Jenna,' I said when she picked up.

There was a long pause.

'Hi. I got your e-mail. Sounds like things are working out for you.'

'It's cool here,' I fibbed.

'We are thinking of coming down for this Netherby

Festival that you mentioned. Rebecca's brother, Justin, says he'll drive us if we pay for the petrol.' Her voice brightened up. 'Jackson says hello.'

'Sounds like you and Jackson are getting on.'

'He's always talking about you, Jenna.' There was a sulky tone in her voice. 'He thinks you're ace for the way you've dealt with things.'

'That was a temporary deal. You promised.'

'I know,' Mia snapped back. Then she explained, 'Mum has been a total pain. Most of my free time is "planned" with activities, tutors or dancing lessons. I have to be in by half past eight. I'm only allowed to go to Rebecca's house. As soon as Dad comes back from his trip to the States, I'll sort things out.'

'Please hurry, Mia. I don't think I can handle it for much longer,' I said in a pathetic voice. Not my style at all. That business with the vase had shaken me up.

'I have to go, Mum's due back soon. Give me the number of the phone box and I'll call you at seven o'clock tomorrow. I want to hear more about that mystery boy.' Mia ended the call.

As I was making my way to the treehouse it began to drizzle and I could feel the fine rain soaking through my hair and cardigan. I wished I'd thought to pick up my coat.

It was five to three and Aurora was waiting for me by her tree. She waved and smiled when she saw me. At least *some-body* was pleased to see me. We walked up to the back of Netherby Hall. The architecture was plainer and tattier than the front of the hall. It was still impressive, though. The rain ran through an ornate lead pipe next to the well-worn back door. Aurora lifted a heavy latch that led us into a tiled porch and then on into a small, warm kitchen.

'Shitty weather, isn't it,' she said as she closed the door behind me.

'Language, Aurora!' came a tired voice from the kitchen.

'But Mum, *you* said it. Just before I went to collect Jenna you said "shitty weather".'

Aurora's mum wiped her hands on a cloth and smiled at me. She was a small woman with long grey hair tied into plaits like Aurora's. She was wearing a nylon overall. She looked more like a lady of the school dinner variety than a lady of the manor.

'Hi, Jenna. I'm Isobel. The quiche will be ready in five minutes. I hope you like field mushrooms,' she said, a worried expression on her face.

'I love them,' I said brightly, despite the fact that I had no idea what a field mushroom was.

'How is Sarah?' she asked. 'It's so good of you to help out in the shop whilst Kai's away. I hope he'll be back soon. He is such a wonderful poet! Sensitive souls always suffer in everyday life.'

I just nodded. Why did Kai take in women so easily? As far as I could make out, he was about as sensitive as a bucket of mud.

Aurora tugged at my damp sleeve. 'Come on, Jenna, I'll show you around.'

We walked back into the gallery. I remembered the last time I'd been there with Gabe. Where was he now? Had he remembered that I was coming?

Aurora threaded her arm through mine and said, 'In the olden days people used to walk up and down this gallery for exercise. Especially when it was too cold or muddy outside.'

I stopped briefly at the picture of Septimus Netherby. 'They could walk past all their dead relatives and nod and say hello.'

Aurora giggled. 'They could stick their tongues out or give them a wink.'

'Or see where they got their cruel eyes or big nose,' I added as we walked along. I stopped again next to the large Chinese vase filled with Gabe's white roses and looked at a picture I hadn't noticed the last time.

It was a tiny portrait tucked away behind the vase. It was a portrait of a beautiful chestnut horse and resting her head against it and smiling was Lavinya.

Aurora looked at the picture, tightened the grip on my arm and said in a tight, hard voice, 'Shitty, evil bitch!'

'Aurora,' I said, shocked. 'Isn't that Gabe's mother? You shouldn't call her names.'

'Why not?' Aurora looked at me and said in a slow venomous voice, 'I hate her.'

'Whoah!' I said taking a step away from her. I was really shocked by the force of her feelings.

'She hurt Gabe and I'm glad she's dead!' Her mouth tightened and small bubbles of foam gathered at the side.

Before I could say anything, Isobel appeared in the doorway and called us back to the kitchen. 'Quiche's ready. Come quickly!'

Chapter Fourteen

Aurora had spooked me. I hadn't seen an expression of such pure loathing like that outside of a horror movie. It was shocking to meet a child who hated a dead person so much. Maybe Lavinya had gone mad. I'd heard a lot of aristocrats do, and she had then tried to hurt her son. It wouldn't be the easiest of topics to 'casually' bring up with Gabe.

We sat round a large wooden table in the kitchen. Aurora didn't seem at all fazed by her outburst and I didn't speak much over the meal. Fortunately I had a large chewy mushroom to deal with, which kept me busy for ages. There was still no sign of Gabe.

The back door rattled and a tall gangly figure, wearing the grubbiest pair of trousers I'd ever seen, came in.

Aurora frowned. 'Daddy, where have you been? Jenna has come to tea.'

He winked at me and kissed her. 'Sorry, Button, but the car broke down again.'

'Poor show!' Aurora tutted. 'And now it's raining.'

'Can't blame me for that. Though come to think of it I did get a spot of cramp this morning. Maybe the gods mistook my stomping for a rain dance.' He began to laugh.

Aurora's fist landed on the table, causing one of the mush-rooms to leap off my plate.

'You'll just have to do a sun dance now, then, if that's the case!'

Without batting an eyelid Lord Netherby unhooked a yellow wok from the wall and began dancing around the kitchen. Isobel grabbed a torch from the shelf and began to switch it on and off.

'Let the sun shine!' she sang in a high-pitched voice.

Hugh Netherby joined in, singing, 'Oh yeah,' and they danced round the kitchen.

It was very funny in an insane-family sort of a way. It reminded me of our 'Must Have Chocolate Now' song. Mum, Marcus and I made it up and we sang it when we were hungry, tired or miserable.

A loud crash of thunder sounded followed by a heavy blast of rain that sent a chill across the kitchen.

'You've been doing it all wrong!' Aurora wailed.

'No problem,' I said. 'Just do the dance backwards.'

'Great idea!' Hugh bellowed and waved the wok in the opposite direction and sang, 'Shine sun the let!'

Hilariously, the rain did ease off a little and we all cheered. There was the sound of a car pulling up outside. Was it Gabe at last? No. Turned out to be Mrs MacLean from the chemist's. She shook off her headscarf and was carrying a large white plastic bag.

'Just dropping off the prescription – ' she said. Then she looked up and saw me, looked flustered and added, 'And some bit and bobs that you requested.' She put the carrier bag down in the hall and left quickly.

When we had all finished eating, Hugh offered to make us

coffee. It took ages, as he was making it the Ethiopian way. He burned some coffee beans in what looked like an old tin can with a handle. We all had to sniff the aroma. Then he disappeared for ages before coming back with a strange black bottle and some tiny cups on a tray. He poured out the thick black liquid. It tasted like liquorice.

'Cardamom,' Isobel said. 'Good for the digestion.'

The coffee wasn't bad and I helped myself to another cup. Aurora got out a battered game of draughts and we all started to play. Another half an hour or so passed and the door opened and Gabe came in.

He didn't see me at first because he was in the porch taking off his Wellington boots. His hair was wet and drops of rain ran down the side of his face. He picked up the carrier bag from the chemist. He barely even looked at me.

Then he walked into the kitchen, put the kettle on and made himself a drink with his back to me. The jumper he was wearing was soaked. I could smell a mixture of wool fibres and his body as the heat in the kitchen warmed him up.

Isobel sipped her coffee. 'You're late,' she said in a disapproving tone. 'The food is cold and we have a guest.'

Gabe stuffed the last piece of mushroom quiche into his mouth in one go and muttered something that sounded like, 'Things to do.'

Had he deliberately stayed away because he knew I was going to be there? I swallowed the rest of the coffee. Some grounds stuck in my throat like sand.

As he reached the door his eyes swept over to mine.

'Hi,' he said in a tone of voice that sounded like he didn't know my name or even cared to find out. Like our night-time meeting had never happened. His features were arranged into a completely different expression.

I lost the next three games. I couldn't work it out. I know he wanted to keep things private, but his coldness towards me went way beyond that.

Aurora looked up from the game and asked, 'Will Sarah be doing her poetry tombola again at the festival?'

'I expect so,' I said.

'I'm thinking of doing my doughnut stall. I should make tons of money.' Aurora's eyes lit up. 'And Gabe will be playing with his band.'

'Quite a family affair, what,' Hugh Netherby said, rubbing his hands.

'I'll probably be back in London by then,' I said, wishing I was already there.

Chapter Fifteen

My head was buzzing. How *dare* Gabe blank me like that! It might be an aristocratic thing to be so rude, but I wasn't going to take it. Not from someone who seemed to like me.

Sarah and I were sitting together in the lounge. Every now and then my eye would just happen to glance at the clock. At five to nine, Sarah said, 'Kai knew how much that vase meant to me. He even wrote a poem about it!' She nibbled the skin at the edges of her fingernails.

I asked, 'Does he make any money from his poems?'

Sarah smiled at me like I was a three-year-old who had asked if the moon was really made of green cheese. 'Kai is not materialistic. He is devoted to his art. We get by. We can usually make a fair bit at the festival.'

'With a poetry tombola?'

'No, it's the food stall that makes the serious cash. I'm going to stuff vegetables into tortillas and call them "Soul Food wraps".'

I glanced at the clock and said as casually as I could, 'I'm going outside for some fresh air.'

Sarah stood up. 'A great idea. I'll come with you.'

'I had sort of arranged to meet up with someone.'

'It wouldn't be one of those boys from next door, would it?' Her voice had a gooey quality.

I nodded. The first time I had clapped eyes on Gabe he had been next door, so it wasn't a total lie.

'I knew it! Don't be late. And wrap up warm,' Sarah squealed.

My aunt was a romance addict through and through. Learn from this, Jenna, I told myself. Do not allow yourself to be taken in by Gabe. It was probably a good thing that Sarah didn't have any children of her own. No way would Mum have let me set foot out of the house at this time of night without good reason.

When I got outside I suddenly started to question myself. What was I doing going there in the first place? After the way he'd reacted earlier, there was every chance that he wouldn't be there and I'd have to huddle in a dark corner for an hour or so to save face before crawling back inside. Or maybe he'd be all over me – full of explanations and crass excuses and trying to kiss me.

My head was buzzing as I stepped out of the house and made my way to the spot where we had met the night before.

He was waiting for me. He held out his hand to me and whispered, 'Sorry about earlier. I'm just no good in public.'

We walked in silence across the fields towards Aurora's treehouse. Then I turned on him. 'Your family is hardly public. The village hall is public. The Mini-Mart is public.'

'I love the way your mouth puckers up when you say public.'

'Would a simple smile and hello have been too much?'

'Way too much. I want to get to know you without any pressure. So, was the mushroom quiche to your liking? Found it a bit chewy myself.'

'You remind me of a field mushroom.'

'Because I'm wild and tasty?'

'Because you're nowhere to be seen during the day, then you spring up from nowhere during the night, you fungus!'

We were both laughing by now. It's hard to hate someone who makes you laugh.

Gabe sighed. 'I don't like my dad and Isobel knowing all my business.'

'So meeting me is business, is it?' I put on a dodgy South London accent.

Gabe put on an even worse one, 'As a matter of fact you are, darlin'.'

I sat down on the grass. 'I can see what a drag it is living in a place where everybody knows what you're up to.'

'Think they know,' Gabe corrected me. 'I hate it when people make assumptions about who you are.'

I thought about Sarah and the vase and how quickly she had judged me. It had been the same at school and with Mia's mum. They had all assumed that it was me.

'It must be hard living in such a small village. Gabe, I won't ever make assumptions about you. I promise.'

'That means a lot to me, Jenna.' Gabe's voice quivered as he spoke.

I looked up. It was a clear night sky full of sprinklings of stars as if someone had shaken glitter over a piece of navy-blue silk.

'Can we just keep meeting each other in the evenings? Take things slowly and keep it private? Can this be our time, Jenna?' Gabe whispered. He was leaning against a tree trunk looking up at the stars.

So I ignored all those sinking doubtful feelings lying in the pit of my stomach and mentally scrunched up the common sense questionnaire that my brain had drafted. Gabe was a risk I wanted to take.

'Yes, this can be our time,' I replied.

Gabe let out a loud yell and ran around the tree.

'So will you be Lord Netherby one day?' I curtseyed in front of him.

He reached out a hand to grab me 'Maybe. Would you like to be a lady?'

I pulled away. 'Thought I was one already.'

Gabe reached over and tugged at my hair. 'A foxy lady.'

'They kill foxes round here, don't they?'

'Only if they don't behave themselves.'

He tugged at my hair again and I got my revenge by ruffling his hair and running off. It took him ages to catch up with me and when he did, he was breathless.

'Maybe being forced to do PE three times a week does pay off.' I laughed as Gabe sat down on a bench and his breathing began to steady.

'Had a bug last week. It's taken a while to shift. We aristo-crats are very delicate creatures, you know.'

I sat down beside him. He put his arm around me.

'I know. Going to the chemist is beneath you. Mrs MacLean makes personal deliveries to your place!' I joked.

He didn't joke back as I'd expected. I felt his arm stiffen and the atmosphere between us changed.

After a long, awkward silence, I stood up and said, 'I should be making a move.'

Gabe pulled me back. 'Stay a bit longer. It's a beautiful evening.'

I sat back down again. The air smelled clean and crisp like

freshly washed sheets. It wasn't spiced with petrol fumes like at home.

'There's so much more sky here,' I said. 'It makes you feel small.'

'Plato says that astronomy compels the soul to look upwards and leads us from one world to another.'

'And I just thought they were pretty, twinkly things!'

'They're much more than that. They are different colours, for one thing.'

'They all look silver to me.'

'If you look at them through a telescope you can see that some are orange or yellow or red, depending on their surface temperature.' Gabe looked back at me. 'Did that sound as nerdy to you as it did to me?'

I stretched out my hand. 'Come on, you old wreck. I'll give you a hand up.'

I braced myself like a muscle man about to lift a truck. He played along and resisted my grip. When he was almost upright he relaxed and fell against me. Instinctively I put my hands out and we found ourselves in an awkward hug.

'Sorry, cheesy move,' he said.

'Pure Gorgonzola,' I replied, enjoying the feeling of his cheek next to mine.

The moment was broken by the sound of Gabe's watch beeping. In a quick change from mush to matter of fact, he said, 'Got to go. Same time tomorrow?'

I nodded in agreement and sighed. 'It's time we went back. Even Sarah must be thinking it's getting late by now.'

It was like we were skimming the surfaces of each other. It felt like we were both holding back from telling each other things. All of a sudden I felt ashamed. When Mia rang me tomorrow I was going to *make* her do the right thing. If Gabe knew why I was here, what would he think of me?

Chapter Sixteen

Mia had said that she would call me that night, so I waited by the phone box. I was determined to have it out with her.

It was amazing how busy the Mini-Mart was. There was a constant stream of cars and vans pulling up, slamming their car doors and then pulling away with their last-minute shopping.

I bought myself a bag of crisps and a magazine and tried to stay calm. The sky was overcast, but it was unbearably hot and airless. I scraped my hair back into a ponytail, but my head still felt hot and itchy.

To stretch my legs I walked over to the front of the shop to drop my crisp packet in the bin. Mia was five minutes late so far.

A group of boys then cycled up to the front of the shop. I recognised them as the scouts from the summer fête. One of them nodded in my direction. I'd promised to save him any Batman comic books that I came across in the shop.

Hugh Netherby was the next customer. He screeched into the car park and jumped out of his battered old Land Rover. He gave me a big wave. Actually it made me feel good knowing that I was a part of a place.

After fifteen minutes, I checked out the phone. It seemed to be working.

A breeze had now begun to blow, but it was no cooler. I could feel itchy lines of sweat drawing down my back.

Then a car pulled up and the occupant, a large man in a loud shirt, walked over to the phone box.

He was on the phone for an agonising twelve minutes. What if Mia had called? Would she try again? Why didn't I just ring her? The thought of her mum answering put me off that idea. I didn't even know what I was going to say to her. She had all the power. If our friendship meant anything to her she'd keep her promise. I'd kept mine to her. And if she didn't, what was the worst thing I could do to her? I could only really threaten to tell Mum the truth. Mia would get mad and things always got worse when Mia got angry. A large chunk of my time spent with Mia was taken up with keeping her sweet. I could see that now so clearly.

The wind had whipped itself up another notch and the sky was darkening. Even an urban urchin like myself had worked out by then that a storm was brewing. The hot, sticky atmosphere was becoming unbearable. I decided to wait five more minutes.

It wasn't all Mia's fault that she was used to controlling situations. She wasn't used to people saying no to her. She was surrounded by people that her parents paid to say yes to her every demand. I had been guilty too of handing my life over to her to control.

Well, I certainly wasn't going to tell her about Gabe. I was scared that if I spoke about him it would jinx things between Gabe and me. Somehow Mia would find a way to spoil it.

There was a lightning flash, followed by loud thunder that released a relentless bead curtain of rain. I ran across the lane and ducked back inside the phone box. There was no way I was going to shelter in the Mini-Mart and miss the call. I wanted to make her finally understand that she had to speak out about what we had done.

The rain instantly brought the temperature down and I began to shiver. A white van chugged round the corner and stopped by the phone box. The window wound down and Charlie popped his head out.

I opened the door of the phone box. 'I was expecting a call, but I was late and missed it and got soaked,' I lied.

Charlie smiled. 'Would you like a lift? I have to drop some stuff off at the village hall first. You can use my phone.'

I shook my head as I jumped into the seat next to him and tried not to soak it too much.

'There's some clothes in the back. You could get changed when we get to the hall. Gabe always leaves something behind him,' he said, chuckling.

'Maybe he's used to servants picking up stuff after him.' I snorted.

'Not Gabe, he's just a natural airhead.'

'How did you two meet?'

'At a pub in Clerkenwell in London. We were watching some anti-folk acts and we got talking. We both were huge fans of Lyle Hasslett and his band, the Stale Pumpkins, so decided to start a band of our own.'

'The Stale Pumpkins? I don't know them,' I said.

'I'll burn you a CD. Lyle has a great voice. We've played with him a couple of times. We called ourselves Goats in a Spin after some lines in one of his songs:

I've put up with your screwball comedy and crackpot
   psychology
So that you would stay with me.

Girl, you've got me dancing like a goat in a spin.
A goat in a spin.'

Charlie had a sweet voice. He finished singing, blushed and said, 'Girls are a bit of a mystery to me.'

'I really liked the tune,' I said in the most un-mysterious tone I could.

Charlie went on. 'That's the great thing about anti-folk music. It's the music that matters. It was Lyle who got us a slot playing at the Netherby Festival. When Gabe told us his family lived in Netherby we thought it would be a great place to spend the whole summer. Our parents were cool about it because they used to go to the Netherby Festival. Gabe's old man said he'd keep an eye on us.'

The van pulled into the empty car park of the village hall.

'Jenna, you couldn't stay for a bit and give me a hand setting up? Only Freddie is nowhere to be seen.'

'No problem,' I said. Sarah had gone over to Julius's to check out some books that were for sale on the internet so she would be ages. I picked up Gabe's green T-shirt and headed for the toilets.

'It'll only take me a minute to get changed out of this wet shirt.'

The T-shirt still smelled of Gabe.

Most of the band's stuff was stored in a cupboard at the back of the hall. Charlie had already made a start getting it out.

'What time does the rehearsal start?' I asked.

'Not for another hour or so, but I wanted to come early and try out some of the equipment.'

After we had set up Charlie began fiddling around with the sound system.

'Test out the mike for me, Jenna?' he called from across the hall.

I blew into it a few times and did the old chestnut thing of saying, 'Testing, testing, one two three.'

It was strange holding a microphone. Too tempting not to try it out. It reminded me of when I was singing in the choir concert and was given a solo in the Christmas concert last year. When Charlie popped out to the van for the hundredth time a song that was one of Mum's favourites sprang into my mind: 'Because the Night', sung by this amazing punk singer/poet called Patti Smith.

I let my imagination fill in the background music and I started to sing. It felt as good as the time I'd had the big cry under the tree. I let my voice go raw and I thought about Gabe.

... *Because the night belongs to love* ...

I stopped and laughed and bowed to my imaginary audience. Someone clapped.

Freddie, Charlie, Gabe and Cleo were staring.

Chapter Seventeen

'So, how do you feel about Charlie asking me to be in the band?' I asked Gabe that evening. We were lying on our backs in a field looking up at the stars.

'Look, Jenna – there's the Plough. It's also known as Ursa Major or the Big Dipper.'

'Answer the question, Gabe,' I said. 'Do you mind me being in the band?'

'You've got an amazing voice,' he said, after a long pause.

'Answer the question,' I insisted.

'It'll be good for the sound of the band to have some extra backing vocals. Lots of music people come to the festival to look for new talent.'

'Gabe.' I sat up and prodded him. 'Tell me how you feel about it.'

He lifted his arms up in a mock defensive way. 'OK, OK. It feels a bit weird.'

'Because of Cleo.' My mouth felt dry. She had gone up the wall when Charlie had suggested that I sing on a couple of songs they were planning to perform at the festival.

Gabe sighed. 'Partly because of her, but mainly because I'll find it hard to keep my hands on my drum sticks when you're around.'

'What is the deal between you and Cleo?' I asked.

Gabe sat up next to me. 'We are really close friends.'

'Have you ever – '

'We did *try* going out very briefly, but it didn't work out. I feel a lot for her, but I don't feel that way about her. It's a corny thing to say, but we are more like brother and sister.'

This was not what I wanted to hear. I wanted Gabe to say how little she meant to him. It was clear how she felt about him. But he wasn't the type of boy to tell me what I wanted to hear. He was giving me the truth.

'How did you get to know her in the first place?' I asked.

After a long pause Gabe said, 'We have a sort of mother connection.'

'They were best friends or something?' I was probing for more information.

'They both died.'

I stopped. This was the first time that Gabe had spoken about his mother. All I knew about her was that she was a wild spirit and how much Aurora hated her.

'I've seen a photograph of her. She was incredibly beautiful. She was called Lavinya, wasn't she?'

Gabe hunched up his legs and grasped them tightly in his arms. 'She was.'

I put my arm round him, but he felt stiff and didn't respond.

'Was she in some kind of accident?' I asked.

'She was killed by a cruel accident of fate.' Gabe sighed and roughly rubbed at his cheeks. Then he sprang to his feet, stretched like a cat and changed the subject.

'So, Jenna. What about you? I bet you've left some boy pining away for you in London. I'm only your fling for the summer holidays.'

'Some fling. You're too much like hard work!'

Gabe laughed.

'Answer the question,' he said.

'There was a boy, Jackson, and we did sort of hang around together.'

For a split second I was tempted to try and make Gabe feel jealous. Then I glanced up at him. Hadn't he been hurt enough? Much as I was angry with my mum I don't know what I'd do if something happened to her.

'I did really like him. We got on well together. I liked the look of him. Other girls liked him. So it was good for the old self-esteem to get some attention. He made me laugh. Trouble was that my best friend, Mia, liked him too.'

'The best woman won,' Gabe said.

I shook my head. 'You don't know Mia. She's my best friend, but she has her flaws. Mia doesn't do second best. Most of the time I admire her for having that attitude, but things got pretty ugly before I came here.'

'You got expelled from school,' Gabe said quietly.

'How did you know?'

'The Netherby gossip hotline. We were all waiting to see what this brat niece of Sarah's was going to be like. You were supposed to form a gang and terrorise the streets. Or at the very least turn all the young people into delinquents.'

'Thanks, Sarah,' I said. My face and neck burned.

'Don't blame her. She probably didn't say much at all. People have a habit of filling in the gaps by themselves. Netherby folk are famous for their over-active imaginations.'

I buried my head in my lap. 'I feel terrible. I'll have to leave. I can't bear the thought of everybody knowing about me!'

'You can't leave now, Jenna,' Gabe said.

'Why not?'

After a long pause he said, 'Because you're in a band now.'

'Is that the only reason?'

'You can't let Goats in a Spin down. People are counting on you to be around for a while.'

Chapter Eighteen

We met every evening between nine and ten o'clock. There weren't many people around Netherby at that time and the light was fading. Over the next two weeks I learned that Gabe liked hot baths, cold sheets and that he was passionate about the planets and stars. He had been studying A-levels at a college in London, but was going to move to Netherby Community School. He hated people who mix up astronomy and astrology and ask him about star signs. He even showed me his astronomical notebook, where he records all his sightings of stars.

'Now that *is* nerdy.' I laughed, flicking through the notebook.

He stuck his tongue out at me. 'It's called being methodical.'

'Shouldn't you be concentrating on the other kind of stardom?' I handed the notebook back to him. 'The one that comes with record deals and music awards?'

Gabe shook his head. 'Wouldn't be anti-folk if we did that. Not that I'd complain if we did get some attention, actually. Charlie is the real genius. I just back him up.'

I told him about my love for banana and honey toasted sandwiches and my irrational hatred of pickled onions – how it felt like I was eating eyeballs. I showed him the postcards Marcus had sent me from Florida. I confessed about my passion for watching cartoons, my love of picking my toenails and my secret wish to be able to snowboard, but I didn't tell him what happened with Mia and Jackson. I told him I was looking for a new school to go to in about five weeks' time.

Meeting at night made me feel less nervous around Gabe. I didn't have to worry about how I looked, whether I was going red or if my hands were jerking about too much when I was speaking. Mia would always advise me about stuff like that. 'Oh, Jenna, your body language is such a giveaway,' she'd say.

Gabe and I held hands, hugged and laughed a lot. I was often seized by an overpowering urge to kiss him. One time, we were looking over his astronomical notebook and I was sure Gabe was going to kiss me. I leaned forward in anticipation, but we just bumped heads and I laughed it off with some stupid joke about really seeing stars now.

I held back from trying to kiss him after that. I was afraid of being rejected and at the same time terrified of *not* being rejected. I knew that one kiss would never be enough. It was scary to think where it might lead. I'd never felt this on edge about kissing Jackson. I'd felt excited about kissing him, but with Gabe I felt scared as well as excited. Kissing Gabe would feel something like telling him I loved him.

Cleo was always lurking in the background. I couldn't quite shake off the feeling that Gabe wasn't being completely open with me about their friendship.

One evening we were lying on our backs in the treehouse, sharing a headset and listening to music, when she called out his name from beneath the tree.

'You stay here and keep quiet. I'll go down,' he whispered to me.

I strained to overhear their conversation, but they moved away so it was hard. I could only catch the sound of Cleo's laughter. We changed the location of our meeting place for a few nights after that.

I told him things that I'd never told anyone before such as how I'd been insanely jealous when Marcus was born and how I had tried to give him away to an elderly neighbour. Her dog had just died and I said she could have Marcus instead to keep her company.

Gabe told me about how Aurora had swapped a priceless family portrait for a Barbie doll.

'She was furious when Dad made her trade them back.' Gabe laughed.

'I wouldn't like to cross Aurora when she's in a temper,' I said, without thinking.

'Aurora can be a bit of a brat at times, but she's generally OK in company. What did you do to upset her?'

'I was looking a picture in the gallery that she didn't like,' I said quietly as I tried to think of a suitable story to fob him off.

In the end I spluttered, 'It was a picture of your mu . . . a picture of Lavinya.'

'Go on. What did she say?' Gabe's voice rose slightly.

'Er . . . nothing much. I think she was just winding me up,' I said, growing more flustered.

Gabe snapped, 'WHAT DID SHE SAY?'

'She said that she didn't like her very much. I expect she was just jealous or something.'

'Why would she say that?' Gabe's voice was now a mixture of hurt and anger.

'She'd got some silly notion in her head that your mum had

tried to hurt you,' I said, trying to make my voice sound light and desperately regretting not keeping my mouth shut.

To make matters worse it started to rain. Gabe picked up a stone and hurled it roughly across the field.

'Rumours and whisperings can poison your life,' he told me. 'My mum was the gentlest, kindest person on this planet. She was beautiful, Jenna. Not in a superficial way. She was beautiful inside. She taught me a lot about how to live and how to die gracefully.' His voice cracked with emotion.

Then his voice changed again and he said sharply, 'Keep your nose out of my business, Jenna.'

And he stormed off.

I chased after him. 'Don't you dare speak to me like that and then walk away!' I yelled. 'If anyone has the right to walk away it's me!'

Then I stormed off and Gabe chased after me. He grabbed hold of my arm and shouted, 'Stop looking at me like that!'

'What do you mean? You're not making any sense, Gabe. I wasn't looking at you. I was walking away. So get your facts right.' I pushed some wet hair out of my face. It was now raining quite heavily.

He placed his other hand on my shoulder as though he was going to shake me. He leaned in towards me as if he was about to speak. I braced myself for more shouting, but instead he kissed me firmly on the lips. The first attempt was slightly off target and caught the side of my mouth. He gently touched the side of my face and I turned my head and pressed my lips to his. Bits of my hair got tangled up in the kiss and I had to steady myself against Gabe otherwise I would have fallen over. I felt his soft wet cheek and the rough bristles on his chin. His lips felt dry and clumsy on mine at first. But . . . as I returned his kiss I forgot all this as my head swam with the sensation.

I'm not sure how long the kiss lasted. It was a minute at the most. Then Gabe let go of me as abruptly as he'd grabbed me. I put my hand on his chest. He blinked, half-smiled and walked away.

Neither of us said anything.

The next morning there was a small white rose on my bedroom windowsill.

That evening we spent the whole hour standing together in the middle of a field. I stood behind Gabe with my arms round his waist with my face pressed against his back. I followed the rise and fall of his body, as he breathed. Neither of us spoke.

It was that night that I knew for sure that I had fallen for him.

Chapter Nineteen

I didn't feel awkward any more when I was alone with Gabe, but things were the complete opposite when we met for band rehearsals. At rehearsals, Gabe always arrived late and was distant with me, for one thing. Freddie was too absorbed in himself to notice. If it weren't for Charlie, I think I would've stopped being in the band. He was always warm and friendly. He often gave me a lift home in the van.

One time he invited me out for a pizza and I had to make up some lame excuse because it would mean missing my time with Gabe. He just looked confused, shrugged and said, 'OK.'

For another thing, I was acutely aware of Cleo watching my every move. Any attempt at friendship that I made was either brushed off with an insincere smile or a sarcastic comment. Worst of all were the times she just looked incredibly hurt.

After one rehearsal when we were left alone in the village hall I was convinced she was about to lunge at me. Luckily Charlie came back for some electrical lead and she pretended to flick off some thread from my neck.

That evening when we met up, Gabe didn't want to talk about Cleo.

He just said, 'She's a good friend and very protective of me.'

'The opposite of how she feels about me.' Then I told him about how she'd launched herself at me.

'She knows that I'm hiding something from her and she doesn't like it. I'm even thinking of telling her. Would you mind?'

'Are you serious? If she hates me now, she'll go ballistic when she finds out.'

Gabe nodded in agreement. I felt a pang. What was it with this friendship between Gabe and Cleo?

Sarah didn't question my evening walks. One time she did ask me if I was drinking or getting up to no good. Straight after she'd said it she blushed and told me to ignore her. She also half-heartedly said, 'I'm pretty sure that I can trust you, Jenna.'

She hadn't mentioned the vase incident again, but I got the feeling that she still believed that I was behind its disappearance. It had been over a month since Kai's visit and she veered between total misery and outrageous optimism. She offered to pay me for my work in the shop, but I refused, knowing how little money she took in.

At the beginning of August, Mum and Marcus came back from holiday and Mum and I were back on speaking terms. We mostly communicated through e-mail and the occasional phone call from Sarakai. Sarah hadn't got the phone reconnected at the cottage, saying that it was more important for the phone in the shop to be reconnected first.

Mum and I even managed the occasional joke. She sent me an e-mail telling me that it was hard having no one to moan at or blame for things. I sent one back telling her that a month was the usual time for anti-wrinkle creams to start working. All those lines I'd given her must be smoothed away by now.

She told me that she'd need double-strength Botox to do that!

I was happy to leave my old life behind for a while. I did miss Mum and Marcus, but it was good to have a break from Mia and Jackson. I found I was worrying less and less about when Mia was going to speak out. I was beginning to suspect it wasn't going to happen at all. When her dad came back from the business trip she'd probably dream up another reason for not speaking out.

All I really cared about at the moment was Gabe. Every night just before we had to leave one of us would pull the other closer for a kiss. Spending time with him, talking to him and kissing him were the only things that mattered to me as the Netherby Festival came closer. There were just over three weeks to go.

Chapter Twenty

Gabe was even quieter than usual a few days later, but I didn't notice it straight away. I was too hyped up from an incredible day at the bookshop. An American tourist had come in and bought a complete set of first-edition Dickens novels for the asking price.

When I did notice Gabe's reticence, I put it down to pre-haircutting nerves. Sarah had gone away for the evening to do a poetry reading. The night before, Gabe had asked me to trim his hair for him and I'd blagged it and said I could do it easily and invited him round to the house. My hairdressing practice to date had been on my Barbie doll when I was eight and Marcus when he got some chewing gum caught in his hair. Still, if Ava could do it then so could I.

It was weird being together inside a house. I'd decided to cut his hair in the bathroom, which had seemed a good idea at the time, but the harsh strip lighting was unsettling. Gabe seemed smaller and paler in this unnatural light. Plus the sight of all Sarah's dusty personal toiletries including hair removal cream and tampons was pretty cringeworthy.

I had been looking forward to touching Gabe's soft, dark hair. Lately Gabe had developed this habit of taking a strand of my hair and curling it round his fingers as we talked. If he got agitated about something he would tug at it.

'Sit still!' I commanded. Gabe's legs were still twitching.

'I'm not sure if this is such a great idea,' he said, frowning.

'How can you doubt the skills of a woman who sold the complete works of Dickens today!' I joked as I firmly grabbed Gabe's head and waved the scissors.

'Careful!' he snapped and added darkly, 'And remember I only want the ends trimmed.'

'Relax, then,' I said in a tense voice as I cut my first piece of hair. The scissors made a rough burring noise as it cut through his hair.

Gabe demanded to see how much I'd cut off. He turned to look and on impulse I kissed him.

At first he kissed back and I moved round to continue the kiss. Then he shifted his position on the stool, throwing me off kilter.

'I'm sorry, Jenna,' he said as I struggled to regain my balance.

'No harm done,' I said lightly. There was a strange expression in his eyes. I finished trimming his hair in silence.

Afterwards, he stood up. It was very claustrophobic in the bathroom. I took a step back. Gabe wouldn't meet my gaze.

He muttered, 'I'd better go now. I won't be able to meet up for the next few nights. Got things to do. Plus I'm not sure if we should see each other every single night. Why don't we cut it back a bit?'

The insides of my mouth dried up and my face ached like it always did when I didn't want to cry at a sad bit in a film. 'Sure,' I said. Something about my kiss had obviously turned him off.

As we were walking down the stairs, I managed to say, 'You're right. It was probably a bit much meeting every night.'

At the door, Gabe looked back at me as if he wanted to say something, but he just gave me a sad half-smile and said, 'This is not about you, Jenna. It's my fault. I am screwed up at the moment. My head's in bits.'

I shut the door and when the stinging feeling that was circulating through my body eased a little I made myself a large hot chocolate and lay on my bed, sipping it for a long time stroking Tallulah and trying to work things out.

What was it with Gabe? *He'd* been the one who'd insisted on spending time with me. It was confusing. Deep down I knew that I was in love with him and I knew that Gabe liked me. I could feel it. But he was holding out on me.

I suppose I was holding out on him too. He'd never once asked me about why I was excluded from school. He'd taken me on face value. I sighed. I suppose I was going to have to do the same. I was going to have to be mature and calm about things for once.

Chapter Twenty-One

My good intentions on the calm and maturity front lasted until half past nine the next morning. On my way to the bookshop I spotted Gabe and Cleo together. They were walking towards the railway station arm in arm. I couldn't see Gabe's face, but Cleo was smiling. They didn't notice me.

When they were about halfway down Station Road, Gabe stopped and Cleo put her arms around him. I froze. She was carrying a small bunch of those special white roses.

There was definitely something going on between them. I felt a total fool. I should have realised from the start that I couldn't compete with Cleo. I'd always known that she'd do anything to keep Gabe to herself. But I'd trusted Gabe and thought he'd felt the same about me when all the time he must have been seeing both of us. And I was the one he had to keep a deep dark secret. My self-esteem folded like a house in an earthquake. Landslides of anger filled in the empty space. As I stomped back to town I gritted my teeth and said in Sarah-like fashion, 'What we need is positive action! When do we want it? NOW!'

I went to the café, ordered a large slice of cake and e-mailed Jackson. I told him how much I missed him. Then I sent Mia a message saying that she had precisely one week to do something or I would.

No one was going to push Jenna Hudson around any more!

As I was leaving the café I bumped into Charlie and Freddie.

'Yo, my home-girl!' Freddie exclaimed, grinning.

'Isn't it about time you stopped talking like that? It makes you seem ridiculous,' I snapped.

Freddie looked really hurt and Charlie was stunned.

I wasn't finished yet. 'Charlie, if you're still interested we can go out for pizza tonight. Pick me up at seven.'

I walked off before he could answer.

I spent the rest of the day reorganising the books in the shop. I was ruthless. Everything went into precise alphabetical order.

Julius looked on from the comfort of his chair. He just sniffed and said, 'No room for surprises, then? I always like to stumble on a book that's not quite in the right place.'

'I don't like surprises,' I mumbled and carried on reorganising.

When I got home I carried on the reorganisation in my bedroom. I chucked away the rose that Gabe had left on my windowsill all those weeks ago and that I'd carefully pressed in a book.

I even considered chopping all my hair off, but only got as far as snipping off a few split ends. Picking up the scissors was too much of a reminder about last night.

I never had much time for poetry at school, particularly old stuff, but I was enjoying dipping into *Vintage Verse*. I'd open a page at random and read the poem to myself over and over until the words stuck in my brain. I found a poem to match my mood. It was a sonnet by William Shakespeare. Repeating the last lines over and over made me feel a lot better.

For I have sworn thee fair, and thought thee bright,
Who art as black as hell, as dark as night.

Then I moved the bed and sorted through my clothes. I even attempted to colour-code them, but as I'd only brought five T-shirts and one hoodie, it was a pretty pointless task.

I had just laid out all my clothes on the bed when Sarah knocked on my door and announced, 'Charlie's here.'

I'd completely forgotten about issuing my pizza declaration. I raced downstairs to cancel, but Charlie was wearing a new shirt, freshly washed jeans and no beanie hat. Sarah was asking him about how I was doing in the band. He didn't seem to know what to do with his hands as they moved from his pockets to behind his back to dangling in front of his body.

I didn't have the heart to say I'd made a mistake. So we caught the bus to Netherby.

I wasn't that hungry, but Charlie didn't seem to notice. He kept ploughing through his pizza. As long as I kept asking him music questions, he was quite happy to keep on chatting.

'How's Freddie?' I asked.

Charlie grinned. 'I left him in his room brooding.'

'I was a bit harsh.'

'You were wonderful, Jenna. Your eyes sort of flashed in a scary way. It knocked me sideways, but you've made Freddie sit up and think.'

'I owe him a huge apology. I hope I haven't scarred him for life.'

'He's more scratched than scarred.'

I was beginning to enjoy myself. Charlie was good company. I regained my appetite in time to sample the all-you-can-eat ice cream bar.

The restaurant was small and every table was full. As I

glanced around the room it was no surprise to me now that there were lots of familiar faces. We were sitting opposite the vicar and Sheila, the Netherby Hall tour guide. I wondered what the local gossips would make of that.

On my way to get my third helping of ice cream, I overheard some of their conversation.

'So do you think I should speak to Lord Netherby about my plan, vicar?'

'It's an excellent idea, Sheila, but I should leave it a couple of days.'

'But it'll soon be the festival and no one can contact him then.'

The vicar lowered his voice, making my ears prickle. 'This is delicate, but I'm sure I can rely on your discretion, Sheila.'

Sheila twittered something in response.

'Today is the anniversary of his first wife's untimely death, so I don't think it is proper for you to discuss opening a tea room in Netherby Hall at the moment.'

'Oh, I see.'

And so did I.

Chapter Twenty-Two

I woke up early the next morning. Tallulah blinked and purred at me in delight as I filled her bowl with cat food to stop her meowing and waking Sarah as I sneaked out of the house.

It was a beautiful morning with a light breeze. The air was filled with birdsong. I felt quite chirpy myself. I cut across the field like a regular country person and made my way towards Netherby Hall.

I wasn't exactly sure what was going to happen, but I knew that I had to see Gabe. I didn't want to give up completely on our relationship. Now that I knew about the anniversary of his mum's death, I had to try and understand what he was going through. I couldn't begin to imagine what my life would be like without my mum.

As I walked up the drive I practised what I was going to say. My first idea was to pretend that I'd found a book that Gabe wanted. Then I changed it to a rare record that I'd found that I thought he could give me some advice on. Or would it be better to say it was something to do with Goats in a Spin . . . I was so wrapped up in my thoughts that I didn't notice the sound of a lawnmower chugging away and the smell of freshly mown grass.

I looked to my left and could just make out a familiar dark head bobbing over the hedge. Gabe was manhandling an ancient lawnmower around a large tombstone. He was dressed in his tattiest pair of jean and an old jumper. He badly needed a shave.

'Hello,' I said as I walked towards the lump of stone and traced the inscription with a finger.

Gabe turned off the mower and wiped some sweat off his forehead with his hand. He looked at me warily.

'So this is Septimus Netherby's monument to his beloved Brutus?' I said, remembering the time we'd met in the long gallery. Gabe nodded as he walked over towards me.

'I won't stay long. I just wanted to say that . . .' I fumbled around for the right words. 'It must be hard for you without your mum . . . oh . . . I don't know what to say.'

Gabe traced his little finger along the inscription. *To the memory of a beloved friend who stood by me in fair winds and foul, whose loyalty never wavered and who is greatly missed.*

Our little fingers touched on the stone. I looped mine around his. He squeezed it back. He had tears in his eyes.

'Septimus could write with so much feeling about his dog. I wonder how he would have felt if he'd truly loved another human being,' Gabe said.

'Or been loved,' I added.

'It's been a tough couple of days for me, Jenna. I should be more prepared for it with each year that goes by, but I'm not – I'm always taken by surprise by the force of my feelings. Mum had been through lots of bad patches. Trips to the hospital when I'd prepared myself for the worst thing possible to happen. And it never did. She always recovered. Then when it was a beautiful sunny day and she wasn't feeling bad she just slipped away when I was out at the shops. That's the thing that I can't get over. The way she left me, Jenna. I don't ever want to feel like that again. I just can't bear to get close to anyone and then have it all fall apart again.'

I put my arms around him and held him. I felt closer to him than ever. After a while I said, 'Why don't we play truant for the day? Go off on a big walk or something. I could leave a note for Sarah and make some sandwiches. They'd have to be tomato because that's all we've got in the house.'

'I'd love to.'

We started meeting up again every evening after that.

Chapter Twenty-Three

I was finding out all sorts of things about myself. Who would've thought that I would become an expert haggler? When people brought books in to sell or wanted a discount I would drive a hard bargain. Julius called me 'top notch', which I'm pretty sure is a compliment.

I was reading a lot more too. I had chomped through some old battered Penguin Classics books and a modern cult novel that made more sense when I read it backwards. I had attempted to teach myself Russian, but the accompanying tape had got all chewed up.

One day Ava asked me, 'Don't you miss being in London? When I was fifteen I longed to be a sophisticated city girl.'

For the first time in ages I thought about my life in London. 'I do miss browsing in clothes shops, eating junk food and being in a crowd of people where you don't know anyone.'

'Netherby has its comforts and consolations,' Ava said, smiling knowingly at me.

It was comforting to be there. Sarah would've pined dead away, and Tallulah would've been all fur and bones without my trips to the Mini-Mart to replenish her food. The bookshop would have gone to rack and ruin. And I was singing again. And there was Gabe.

As my relationship with Gabe got deeper so did my interest in *Vintage Verse*. I loved some of the lines by Arthur Symons:

As a perfume doth remain
In the folds where it hath lain,
So the thought of you, remaining
Deeply folded in my brain,
Will not leave me: all things leave me:
You remain.

I'd never realised before how useful poetry could be in expressing how you feel, when ordinary words sounded corny or cheap.

There was also the battered book of quotations. I felt sentimental about it and kept it by me on the counter. 'Music hath charms to soothe the savage breast' being my favourite quotation, of course!

I was enjoying spending time with Ava. She was teaching me the correct way to trim hair and how to do her trademark bouffant hairstyle. She also showed me how to make pom-poms. This had given me a brilliant idea for an art installation. I was going to cover Mrs Kelly's office in pom-poms!

What was I doing planning on going to back to Coot's Hill? Even if they begged me I wasn't going back there. Mum had hinted in her e-mails that she had a few new school options arranged for me, but I hadn't asked her about them. I wasn't ready to think about them just yet. I had a few ideas of my own and I wanted to see how things developed with Gabe.

I was settling down with *Vintage Verse* on a rainy Tuesday morning when the bell rang. I didn't look up at first. I was engrossed in a poem by Ben Jonson. I was particularly taken by the lines:

Join Lip to Lip, and try . . .
Each suck the other's breath,
And whilst our Tongues perplexéd lie . . .

Someone coughed. I looked up and saw it was Cleo.

In a panic, I glanced back at my book to give myself time to think. Maybe she had just come in to browse . . .

'I want a word with you,' she said, her voice as sharp as a stiletto heel.

'Plenty of words around here,' I said, trying to make her laugh. If I could make her smile, then maybe just maybe she wouldn't kill me. I gripped on to the spine of my poetry book.

'Stop bothering Gabe,' she said in a steely voice.

I swallowed and frantically searched my brain for something to say. Bothering? He certainly didn't seem very bothered.

But Cleo was in no mood for an in-depth discussion. She leaned over the counter, jabbed me in the chest and said, 'Leave him alone.'

'Hey,' I said, weakly, as her finger seemed to have super-human powers and knocked me a little off my feet. The high street was deserted. Where were all those prying eyes when you needed them?

I took a deep breath and attempted to get some of my fighting spirit back.

'Isn't that for Gabe to decide?'

Cleo frowned. 'He doesn't *need* you messing him around. I've seen the way you look at him.'

The venom she put into the 'you' was scary. I was a low-life, repellent, foul-smelling scum of the earth.

I forced myself to look in her eyes. Her lips were curled into a sneer, but her eyes had a startled look like she was afraid. I suddenly felt a bit sorry for her.

I decided to try the soft, reasonable approach.

'I know that you and Gabe are friends and I don't want to spoil that.'

Cleo's eyes flashed. 'You haven't a hope in hell of knowing the extent of our friendship.'

'You're right. I can't know what it's like to grow up without a mother.'

Cleo stopped short and spluttered, 'Gabe told you *that*? He had no right telling you. You are totally messing with his head. Wheedling your way into the band so you can be with him. Just back off. Because in the long run, you're wasting your time.'

'My time to waste,' I snapped back and cringed inwardly. This situation was heading into a slapping match and there was nothing I could do or say to stop it.

'Gabe and I have a special bond that you will never have!'

I was literally saved by the bell as Ava walked in. She was wearing a bright pink plastic apron and carrying a large plunger.

'Blocked sink. Thought I'd pop in and check on you, Jenna.' She waved the plunger menacingly in the air and turned to Cleo. 'Everything all right at the café? Backed-up drains can create havoc. Not to mention the smell.' Ava sniffed theatrically. 'There is a faint whiff of something unpleasant in here.'

Cleo treated us both to one more glare and left the shop.

Ava rustled her way towards me, plonked the plunger on the counter and said in a whisper, 'Watch your back with that one. It has claws and sharp teeth.'

'What have I done to her?' I said.

Ava nodded and said theatrically, 'You're young. You're beautiful with a shady past. You're competition.'

I wasn't convinced. Cleo was afraid of something more than just a rival for Gabe's affection.

Chapter Twenty-Four

What if Gabe and I hadn't kept the secret as well as we'd thought? Someone could've easily seen us scrambling up the treehouse or walking through the fields. Cleo was definitely suspicious. She'd been to the treehouse a couple more times, forcing Gabe and me to stay away. Ava was driving me nuts by winking knowingly at me at every opportunity.

But why did it matter so much?

What was it about me that made boys embarrassed to be seen with me? Jackson had always shifted the ground from under my feet. Doing things like texting me all the time, but then never being quite sure if he was available when I suggested we meet up. Or he'd ask me to meet him for coffee and then I'd find out he'd asked Mia and about six of his mates along as well. With Jackson I always felt that I had to impress him to get noticed.

Gabe could be moody, stubborn and totally paranoid about people knowing his business, but when it was just the two of us it was different. I felt that I could be myself again. Maybe, deep down, he was ashamed to be seen with a delinquent like me. Whether he liked it or not he had a position in the community, being the son of Lord Netherby.

As for my shady past, as Ava had put it so dramatically, it was time for me to face facts. Mia was not going to do anything for me. That wasn't how our friendship worked. We were social friends not deep soulmates. Being known as her friend had made my school life easier, but that's all. The sooner I faced up to that sad fact, the sooner I could move on and make some real friendships.

I was left with two choices. I could do something about the situation myself or shut up and live with my bad girl reputation. That really made me think about how easy it is to get a bad label stuck on you. And how hard it is to take it off once people have made up their minds about you.

I was just about to close up the shop when the bell went and Freddie and Charlie ambled in.

Freddie said, 'Bodacious news! With only days to go, the Stale Pumpkins have pulled out of the festival and we have been offered their slot.'

'Is that good?' I asked.

'Does a cat like cream?' Charlie said.

'Does a bear . . .' Freddie began.

'OK, I get the point,' I cut in.

Charlie went on. 'It'll mean loads more rehearsals. Only problem is we can't have the village hall. It's been fully booked up by other festival bands.'

They looked at me like a pair of lost puppies until I cracked and said, 'It'll be a bit cramped, but I'm sure Sarah wouldn't mind us practising here. If we gave her something towards the electricity. Besides, I owe you something, Freddie, by way of an apology for being so rude to you the other day.'

I'd hardly got the words out before Charlie had leaped on to the counter and given me a big kiss. Then he blushed the deepest red I'd ever seen a face go.

'Way to go, bro,' Freddie cheered before he slapped his hand over his mouth and said, 'Oops, what I meant to say was, "What a fantastic idea!"'

Charlie bundled him out of the shop.

As I was mulling this over, the phone rang. I was of two minds whether to answer it or not. I wasn't in the mood for answering book questions. So I put on my snootiest voice. 'Sarakai Books, how can I help?'

'I think the question is more, what can I do for you?'

'Mia, is that you?'

'No, it's her body double speaking.'

'How did you find this number?' I asked.

'Ways and means, ways and means. Look, I can't talk long. Just thought I'd ring to let you know that I . . .'

'You've told the school, I knew you would. What did they say?' My voice went racing on and on.

There was a long pause at the other end.

'It's the summer holidays. There's no one in school at the moment. I was calling you to say that I got your e-mail. A bit threatening for my liking . . . but Jackson and I are coming down to see you. We've got tickets for the Netherby Festival.'

'I thought you weren't allowed to associate with me.' My mouth felt dry.

Mia laughed. 'Justin is driving us down if we pay his petrol money and buy his ticket. Mum hasn't made the connection between you and Netherby.'

'I'm touched at the lengths you'll go to see me,' I said sarcastically.

'I'm borrowing a tent. It should be great fun.'

'I'll be working. I'm running a food stall with Sarah,' I

said. The thought of Mia and Jackson in Netherby unnerved me. Mia and Jackson were part of my London world. They didn't belong here. I was a different person here and I didn't want them to spoil things.

Mia continued chatting. 'I want to hear all about your mystery boy. Or was he just a product of your fevered brain?'

Why had I bragged about Gabe in that first e-mail I sent her? Stupidly trying to impress Mia. I couldn't bear the thought of her knowing about Gabe.

'He's called Charlie and he's really funny.'

'Dying to meet him,' Mia said, then her voice changed. 'Yes, Rebecca, I think you'll find that is the correct use of the apostrophe.'

Her mum must've come into the room. I put the phone down.

After Mia's call I felt unsettled and stifled. I needed a temporary change of scene. I'd heard that there was a cool café in Netherby, so after work I decided that now was a good time to check it out.

Netherby was a smaller version of Greater Netherby. The shops were mainly antique and bric-à-brac. This would've been a much better location for Sarakai Books, I thought.

Every shop window was full of posters advertising the coming festival. One small antique shop had a poster that said: *Boycott Netherby Festival. Keep thugs out of our village!*

So not everybody thought the festival was a good idea, then. As I was staring at the poster something caught my eye. You could hardly miss a large gaudy vase like that. The price tag attached to it was pretty breathtaking too. I rubbed my eyes and looked again.

It was still there.

Chapter Twenty-Five

'I s it better to hurt someone quickly by telling them some bad news or better to say nothing and just wait for them to find out for themselves?' I asked Gabe later that evening. We sat side by side in a corner of the treehouse sharing a bag of cherries.

'If you're thinking of dumping me then I'd prefer to be told right away.' He hurled a bad cherry out of the window.

I told him about seeing the vase in the shop, Sarah thinking I had something to do with it, and my suspicions about Kai having stolen it.

Gabe shook his head. 'Kai can be a bit of a smoothie where the ladies are concerned and his poetry sucks, but I can't believe he's a thief. Besides, he doesn't need to with that valuable record collection of his.'

I nearly choked on a cherry stone. 'Are you telling me that that box of old records is actually worth something?'

'Thousands of pounds. But I don't think he'd ever sell them. He thinks of them as his children.'

'Then why leave them behind?'

'He probably thinks that is the safest place for them whilst he's travelling round for the summer.'

'In the meantime Sarah has to manage the shop alone . . .

She totally refuses to see any of Kai's bad points,' I said.

'What I don't understand is why Sarah assumed that you might have had something to do with it?'

'Because I am a bad girl with a terrible reputation,' I replied bitterly. Then a weird thing happened. Out of the blue, I exploded into tears. A huge volcanic eruption of hot tears and snot completely overwhelmed me.

Gabe just let me get on with it. Then he handed me a crumpled tissue from his coat pocket.

'You can talk to me about it . . . if you trust me.'

I nestled against his T-shirt, breathed in his sweet smell, and considered. I wanted to tell him . . .

'It's not that I don't trust you. Even though I've only known you a few weeks, there's something about you. You're solid. But you're not always open with me and I totally respect that, because I'm just the same and I know how you hate people making assumptions about your life . . . And I want to tell you, but . . . Oh my, I'm babbling on like a total fool.'

Gabe said, 'Who cares? There's no one around for miles. Apart from me.'

'That's the point. I care about what you think of me. I don't want you to think less of me,' I said, my voice getting smaller.

'How do you know that I will?' Gabe looked into my eyes.

I looked down and said, 'Because when I allow myself to think about what I did, I feel so bad that I start gasping for breath.'

Gabe squeezed my arm.

'I don't think I could ever think badly of you, Jenna. People make mistakes, have regrets . . . Sometimes you have to learn to live with them, learn *from* them.'

'Sometimes the mistakes you make can really hurt people. Mum was desperate to get me into Coot's Hill School. It's incredibly hard to get into and I'm not a super-genius or anything. She had to spend a lot of money on a house in the right area for me to be considered. That and my musical ability got me in.'

'I didn't know you played anything.'

'The clarinet, and I sang in the choir at my primary school.'

'You are full of surprises, Jenna. I didn't take you for a choir girl.'

'Not all of them are good surprises . . .' I tried to laugh, but my face felt tight. I was aware that this was my chance to get it off my chest. Find out Gabe's true feelings. Let Gabe know what I was capable of and see how he liked me after that.

'I pretty much hated the school from Day One. The atmosphere was too stuck up and competitive. Life in Year Seven was pretty tough. I didn't know anyone as we'd only recently moved into the area. When I started Year Eight, Mia moved in next door and joined the school. She was fearless and right away she helped me fit in better at school.'

'Having someone to look out for you is important,' Gabe added.

'Then in April, at the start of last term, Jackson arrived. He'd been at my primary school. So for the first time it felt like I had a group of friends. We fell into a habit of mucking around. We all got off on the wrong foot with our new French teacher, Ms Rose. She had a really sharp tongue and a way of looking down her nose at you if you made a mistake. Even Rebecca Worth, a complete swot, struggled with the homework – and she has two brains. I used to like French, but I found myself losing interest and, eventually, confidence.' I looked up at Gabe. He smiled back at me. No matter how many times I swallowed, my throat felt dry. The aftertaste of the cherries in my mouth made me feel sick.

'Ms Rose had arranged a day trip to France. The plan was to leave really early in the morning, spend the day in Calais and return on the ferry in the evening. Mia, Jackson and I were fooling around like we usually did before we got on the coach. Ms Rose threw a huge wobbly, said she had had enough of our rudeness and wasn't going to take responsibility for us on the trip. She told us to report to the head teacher's office. What really put our backs up was the fact that we weren't really behaving any differently than we usually did and she threatened to withhold our trip money. I could tell the other teachers thought she had overreacted, but they didn't say anything.

'So as the coach set off we went back to the classroom. We were really angry. I had been looking forward to the trip for ages. I'd nagged Mum to find the money and now I was going to lose it and I didn't think our behaviour had been any worse than it usually was.'

I looked at Gabe to gauge his reaction, but he was sitting with his head in his hands. He was probably too embarrassed to look at me.

'Instead of reporting to the office we sneaked into Ms Rose's private office and made ourselves a cup of her special French coffee. Then Jackson drew a moustache on one of her posters. Mia found a handbag in a desk drawer. It was a ridiculous pink, fluffy one and we all spent ages posing with it and doing exaggerated impressions of Ms Rose. We were all laughing hysterically. I can't remember the exact order of what happened next, but one of us looked inside the bag and found a credit card. So we sneaked out of school back through the car park. Most people thought we'd gone on the trip. We hopped on a bus to the West End. Jackson said he had heard about an electrical shop that never asked any questions.

'At the time I knew what I was doing was totally out of order, but we kept egging each other along and reminding ourselves that we were only spending our own money after all. We had convinced ourselves that if Ms Rose was going to hang on to our trip money then we deserved some of her money.'

My heart was pounding as I relived that moment.

Gabe could see I was worked up. 'You don't have to tell me any more,' he said.

But I had to carry on. If I stopped now I'd probably never have the courage to talk about it again.

'Mia marched into the shop. Jackson and I watched her through the window. My heart was pounding and everything seemed to be on fast forward. Any second now I kept on telling myself someone's going to find out and stop her. But the bloke didn't seem that bothered on checking the signature and it was all too easy.

'Mia came out with a carrier bag. She had bought a digital camera. When I saw the camera I started to freak out and I kept on saying, "We've got to take it back! We've got to take it back . . ." until Mia slapped me hard in the face. She caught one of her nails in my hair clip and shrieked, "You've broken my nail." That seemed to bother her more than anything.

'Jackson giggled, but then, sensing my state of panic, he turned to me and said that we could always return the camera later. Get the money put back on the card. Then no one would be any the wiser. I cheered up.

'We messed around with the camera and sent the photos to Mia's computer in an internet café. Then we went for an ice cream. Mia volunteered to take the camera back while

Jackson and I waited in the café. We were coming down off the buzz. "That was crazy," Jackson kept on saying. I think he was starting to feel bad. I know I was feeling queasy and the sides of my head throbbed.

'Ten minutes later Mia came back. She handed me the credit card to look after. I shoved it in my pocket. "Get rid of it," Mia told me. "Or am I expected to do everything?"

'We hung about until the end of school. I knew we'd made a terrible mistake. I couldn't throw the card away. I wanted to put things right, put it back in Ms Rose's handbag. After all the camera had been returned, hadn't it? So there was no money actually taken from the card. Ms Rose would think that they'd got her number mixed up.

'I managed to get back into the classroom unnoticed and located the handbag, but just as I had got the handbag open I was spotted by one of the cleaners who told one of the teachers and I was caught.

'I didn't say much at first. I wasn't going to grass Mia and Jackson up. Mum was sent for and I was suspended pending a full enquiry. Mia sneaked round to my house that evening. She was boiling mad. I didn't understand why. "You did take the camera back, didn't you, Mia?" I asked her.

'She didn't answer me – instead she launched an attack on me. "What difference does that make to you getting caught with the card? What an incredibly stupid thing to do. What were you thinking of, trying to put it back?" and so on. She said she didn't mind admitting what she did, but thought we should keep Jackson out of it, because he got in trouble at his last school and was asked to leave. His mum had said she'd send him to school in Nigeria if he got into any more trouble.

'So I agreed to leave Jackson out of it. And he kept his

distance from me at school and I assumed whatever relationship we had was over. That hurt me a lot. But Mia was all smiles and pleaded with me to keep quiet.

'She wanted me to wait until her dad got back from his business trip to the States before owning up. Her mum can be a real terror to deal with. She said he'd be on our side. That he was a whiz at working out deals. And he was always getting into trouble himself when he was at school. Plus he donates tons of money to the school. Then she promised to admit her part when he got back.

'So I took the rap. I admitted that I had taken the credit card and gone shopping with it. I answered all of their questions. I was scared, but also a bit relieved actually. Getting found out helped to ease the anxiety and guilt. I just figured that once Mia owned up too, then I wouldn't feel so isolated.

'The money had not been credited back on the card and Mum had to pay it back. Mia must have lied to me about returning the camera. Mrs Kelly wanted to call in the police, but Ms Rose said no. I said that I'd bought a camera but panicked and thrown it away She just kept looking at me and saying that, as I was so weak and easily led, I had been punished enough. I think she knew that Mia and Jackson were involved too, but she didn't say anything. So I was sent to Sarah's.'

I buried my head in my hands and waited for Gabe to respond. The sides of my head throbbed and my hands shook. I had no idea what kind of reaction to expect from Gabe. Disappointment, horror, disgust, shame maybe. I certainly wasn't expecting what I got.

I looked up. Gabe was smirking and trying to stop himself from laughing!

I stormed off as fast as I could.

Chapter Twenty-Six

'Jenna, stop!' Gabe raced down the hill after me. 'I opened up to you and all you could do was laugh!' I screamed as he tried to grab my arm. I snatched it out of his reach.

'I'm sorry. I wasn't laughing at you. I was relieved. I was really scared that you were going to tell me something horrible. Your mistake is one that can be undone.'

'What do you mean?'

'It's not like you've committed a murder. There's no going back from that, is there? This isn't that bad. You can live this down. But you've been badly let down by your so-called friends.'

'Mia said that she'd speak out just as soon as her dad gets back. He's away on a long business trip to the States. She promised me she would put things right,' I said.

'And you believe her? Mia and Jackson have stitched you up.'

Gabe grabbed me, but I shook him off.

'No, they wouldn't do that to me. I'm their friend,' I insisted, though it was half-heartedly. It was one thing thinking about it and quite another to admit my fears out loud.

'Sounds like that's exactly what they've done. Shown their true colours.'

'I'm not going to get Jackson or Mia into trouble. Jackson would get sent away.'

'He's a big boy. He should take responsibility for his part. He knew about the shop, didn't he? He should have been more careful if he was at risk of being sent away. He's quite happy to see you sent away from home.'

I put my hands over my ears. 'Stop it! You're the first person I've trusted to tell. I wish I hadn't now. Stop being so heartless.'

'But I don't believe that Mia and Jackson are true friends. Or that Mia will ever own up. Maybe she will when the moon turns pink! Believe me, Jenna, I'm not heartless. I seem heartless, but I do have my reasons.'

He grinned and something snapped inside me. I was furious.

'You don't have a heart because you were born like that,' I yelled back. 'Who do you think you are? Mr Perfect? Believe me you're far from that. You're moody and impossible and your obsession with privacy drives me nuts. Do you think you're so special that everyone is dying to know your business? Just because Cleo worships the ground you walk on doesn't mean that the rest of us do. Just because you're an aristocrat doesn't mean that you're any different from me. You have the same blood running through your veins!'

'I was born HIV-positive, Jenna,' Gabe said.

I started to say something, but I froze. It took me a few moments to take in what he'd said. It felt like my stomach filled with ice water.

'What?' I mumbled, too stunned to think clearly and afraid of what he'd say next.

'I'm sorry. No way should I have blurted it out like that.'

Gabe began pacing around. 'In fact, I shouldn't have told

you at all. Big mistake. Really big bad mistake. Just forget you ever heard it. Erase it from your memory . . . what am I saying? It's not like you could do that . . . could you?'

'Gabe.'

That was the only thing I could say out loud. My brain was racing. Gabe couldn't be HIV-positive. AIDS was a terrible disease . . . Oh my God, was Gabe going to die soon?

Thousands of terrifying thoughts swirled round inside my head. The chill in my stomach started to spread through my body, making me suddenly desperate for the bathroom.

Gabe became really agitated. 'Jenna, you can't tell a single soul,' he said, looking fiercely into my eyes. 'This is really important. You've got to promise me not to say anything. Not to Sarah, to your Mum or any of your friends. Not anyone.'

I was still too stunned to speak. Instead I just nodded.

'Swear it. Go on.' There was desperation in his voice. He grabbed my arm roughly and pointed up to the sky.

'Swear on the lives of your family that you won't tell.'

Gabe's eyes were wild.

'By all that I hold dear, I absolutely promise not to say anything.' I tried to make my voice sound convincing, but I was really scared. I was freaked out by what Gabe had told me, but I was also scared of hurting him. Maybe even losing him. Gabe was still pacing about manically in circles.

'I really should be going. I have stuffed up big time here and I'm going to be late taking my meds.'

I took hold of Gabe's hand, ignoring that part of me that kept saying, Should you be doing that – or anything that's close now that you know about him?

I stamped on those fearful thoughts and squeezed his hand tighter.

Chapter Twenty-Seven

My whole body shut down under the weight of Gabe's announcement, and I slept like a log that night. My brain sent me to sleep because it was too afraid to think.

As soon as I opened my eyes it hit me again. My heart began to race. At first I told myself that Gabe was playing some kind of cruel practical joke on me. Or that perhaps I had misheard him. That he had only said he was afraid he might be HIV-positive. He said that he was born HIV-positive, but perhaps he'd grown out of it by now. Babies grow out of illnesses, don't they? Maybe he was some kind of attention-seeking hypochondriac . . . I buried my head under the covers.

I wasn't even sure what being HIV-positive really meant. I knew it was a virus that was spread by unsafe sex or sharing needles. There were tablets that you could take to get rid of it, weren't there? It didn't mean you had to die a horrible death.

I wished I'd listened more in sex education classes at school. Not that Coot's Hill went in for full and frank discussions when it came to sex. Some of the parents and governors had objected to what little advice we were given.

I usually switched off when the issue was raised on the news. It was confusing. Some people said it was an epidemic in

Africa and other people, in the Western world, believed it was an illness that affected only gay people. A lot of people complained about the cost of the drugs. I'd watched a programme about people with AIDS in England, but they were mainly drug users. This sort of thing happened to other people, not to the son of Lord Netherby. Not to Gabe.

I sat up in bed. How could it be affecting Gabe? He didn't look sick. Then another thought struck me. I had kissed Gabe. Did that now mean I could be infected too? You caught AIDS through exchanging body fluids, didn't you? I might have had a cut in my mouth or an ulcer.

I jumped out of bed and raced to the bathroom, where I was horribly sick.

Sarah heard me and brought me a cup of tea in bed.

'It's probably nerves about performing at the festival,' she said. 'I always get nausea before a poetry reading.'

I nodded. Sarah fiddled with her fingers as if her many rings were still there, before continuing, 'I'd make you stay in bed, but if you're up to it, I really need you to open the shop. With the festival starting in a couple of days the place gets really busy and I have a chance to make some real money. I need to pop over to the bank and sweet-talk them into a little loan. Do you mind?'

I shook my head. Working in the shop would take my mind off things for a while.

Gabe was waiting for me outside the house. He looked terrible, like he hadn't slept. He rushed straight over to me.

'Jenna, I'm really sorry. It wasn't fair of me to blurt out something like that.'

I touched his arm. He was trembling.

'Gabe,' I said. It was the only word I could say. Everything else would sound useless or hopeless.

'Do you hate me, Jenna?' His eyes shone with fear.

I shook my head. 'Maybe the world or a stupid virus, but not you.'

He put a letter in my hand. His hands were cold.

'Read this when you're on your own. I have to go up to London to talk to some people in my support group.'

'But it's the rehearsal this evening,' I said and then I did an impression of his voice, 'Don't forget you're in a band. You can't let Goats in a Spin down.' I couldn't bear the thought of him going away at that moment.

'Can I go with you?'

'No, Jenna, you can't. I'll try and get back in time . . . but I'll definitely be back for the gig.' He made as if he was going to kiss me and then he changed his mind when he saw me stiffen. His eyes shimmered with hurt. I looked down at my fingers, which were gripping his letter tightly.

I felt my stomach wrench as I watched him walk away and wondered how on earth I was going to make it through the day.

Fortunately, Julius was in the shop.

'Thought I'd help out with the festival rush. I've dug out some old books on paganism and alternative religions. They always sell well this week.'

That day I appreciated his bad jokes and I tried to share his wild enthusiasm about books. I even tuned the radio to Radio 4.

'Things are looking up,' he said and winked at me.

All the while I was acutely aware of Gabe's letter folded up in my jeans pocket. I was too afraid to read it, especially with other people around. I was terrified of how its contents would affect me. But every now and then I'd reach into my pocket and touch it.

Charlie and Freddie popped in to check out the space for tonight's rehearsal. I couldn't bring myself to tell them that Gabe might not show up.

As the morning wore on, the shop got busier and busier, which only made me feel lonelier. There was still no sign of Sarah. I was a bit relieved about that, because I might have been tempted to break my promise and talk to her. I touched the letter again to remind me to be strong and keep my promise to Gabe.

At three o'clock Julius nipped out for 'a spot of tiffin'. Ava brought me in a sandwich and a milky coffee to 'keep my strength up'. She also kept an eye on the customers whilst I ate it. Until then I hadn't realised how late it was or how hungry I'd become.

I'm not sure whether it was a natural lull in trade or the fact that Ava's stare had chased off the customers for a while, but the shop went back to its usual quiet self. Ava returned to the hairdresser's to do a perm and I was left almost alone. There was one customer left in there with me.

The only sensible thing that Sarah had done in the shop was rig up a large mirror so that you could see round some of the dusty corners in the shop. The lone customer was a tall girl with long straggly hair. There was something vaguely familiar about her. If I hadn't been preoccupied by Gabe's letter then I would have put some more effort into remembering where I'd seen her before.

She spent ages in the tiny Health and Well-Being section. Eventually she crept up to the counter and asked, 'Are those records for sale?'

I looked up from my book and said, 'I'm sorry, they're not.'

She nodded and gave me a satisfied smile as if I'd told her what she'd wanted to hear. Where had I seen her before? I coughed. She turned to go.

'That book is for sale, though,' I called after her, eyeing the bump in her jumper.

The girl blushed and took the book out.

'Er, sorry,' she muttered.

It was called *The Perfect Pregnancy*. I noticed that there was still a bump underneath her jumper that wasn't from a book.

'That's on special offer – only fifty pence,' I said with a smile, ignoring the ten pounds written on the price sticker. I figured this girl needed all the help she could get.

She smiled at me, but her expression immediately turned into a frown as she walked out.

Chapter Twenty-Eight

S arah finally came dashing into Sarakai at around four o'clock. The shop was empty and she was full of apologies. Julius said he'd help her cash up so that I could go home and mentally prepare for the rehearsal that evening.

The weird thing was that the minute I had the opportunity to read Gabe's letter in private, I kept putting it off. First of all I had to make a great fuss over Tallulah and feed her. Then I had to make myself a cup of herbal tea to calm myself down.

I decided to take a long hot bath and get changed.

When all my excuses had run out I curled up on my bed and opened the envelope.

Jenna,

What can I say? I feel so bad for dumping my news on you like that. Please believe me when I say I never planned to blurt it out. I knew I would tell you eventually – part of me has wanted to tell you for a long time. In fact, I'm relieved that you know because now you can walk away. And I can start trying to forget about you.

But I think you deserve to know more about me, so I am writing to tell you about those aspects of my life that I normally keep private.

Seventeen years ago, I, Gabriel Hugh Lawrence Netherby, was born. My mother had run away from Dad following a stupid argument. As well as being beautiful, Mum was also stubborn and impulsive.

She didn't know it at the time, but she wasn't alone.

She ran away to stay with friends in Kenya. Months later, when she realised that she was pregnant, it was too late to travel home. She was one of those people who don't show many signs that they're expecting and she'd put the symptoms she did have down to being in a different country. During the pregnancy there were serious complications and she had a blood transfusion. The blood was contaminated and so we both contracted HIV. This was in the days before they started screening blood.

For a few months after I was born Mum planned to return to England to make it up with Dad and present him with his son and heir.

When she came back to London she went for some routine medical checks and found out that she was infected. Can't begin to imagine how that must feel. Most parents blame themselves for all the little things that happen to their children. So Mum was devastated that I had the virus too. She felt that it was her fault.

She didn't make it up with Dad even though she still loved him. She divorced him to protect him and the Netherby name, and she didn't tell him about my existence for a long time. She stayed in London.

When I was nine I started asking loads of questions about why I was always going to hospital for blood tests and taking pills. She told me that I had some bad bugs living in my blood and that the tablets I was taking *made them go to sleep. When the bugs woke up they hurt me.*

Slowly over the next few years I began to work things out in my head. Mum would get sick or she'd be too tired to get up for days. She had loads of pills to take.

One day I asked her, 'Am I going to die?'

Mum hugged me and said, 'Gabriel, we're all going to die some day.'

A tingle went down my spine as I recalled the day of the summer fête. Gabe had said those same words to me when we were looking at Eveline Netherby's portrait. I had joked about it, saying that I wasn't going to die.

I swallowed hard and continued reading.

Her day arrived a couple of years later when I was eleven years old. My beautiful, brave mother. I miss her more than any words could ever express.

Just before the funeral, Dad found out the reason why she hadn't come back to him. It was hard for him at first because he felt so shut out. He had remarried and had a baby. As far as he knew Aurora was his only child. All that time and he had known nothing about me. When he did find out all about me, he did the honourable thing and took me in.

At first it didn't work out. I was too angry and sad about Mum and he couldn't face up to my illness. So I went to stay with various relatives in London.

Cleo and her mum were the closest thing I had to family at the time. Our mums had been best friends. Cleo has always looked out for me and loved me in her fierce way. I promised Mum that I would always look out for her.

Dad and Isobel didn't give up on me. They kept inviting me to stay and coming to see me. I got to know my baby sister Aurora – who could resist her for long?

My health is such a big part of my life. I get so mad sometimes just thinking about it. Sometimes I feel bitter when I see kids with cancer getting loads of attention, sympathy and support (which, of course, they deserve), whereas I know that those same compassionate people would treat me like I've got the plague or something. In fact that's what they used to call HIV – a plague. Many people see HIV as some kind of divine retribution. They think that people with the virus deserve to be sick. They despise you and are afraid of you. All they see when they look at you is an infection. They forget that you have feelings.

At the moment I am well, because my combination therapy (the cocktail of pills that I have to take every day) is working. I'm happy I've met you, Jenna. Our time together every evening has meant a lot to me. I can relax and be myself when I'm with you, even if I've had to keep this dark secret.

I've always shied away from relationships. But I could never regret the time we've spent together. Apart from Cleo, you are the only girl that I've let myself have feelings for. There's something special about you, Jenna, and over these past few weeks I have fallen in love with you. I don't expect anything in return from you.

By the time you've got this letter I'll be in London. I need to see some people in my support group. I want to spend some time talking things through and I need to be in a space where I feel safe and not judged or pitied.

I'll try not to miss the last rehearsal, but if I do, tell them that I will be there for the festival. We can talk there.

I don't know what you are thinking at the moment, but it's probably for the best anyway if we don't carry on the way we have been doing. I hope we can still be friends. Or that at least you won't think too badly of me.

All that I ask of you is that you don't tell anyone. People can be narrow-minded and cruel, and if the news got out it would seriously hurt my family and me.

Please don't even keep this letter after you have finished reading it.

Love, Gabriel

'What's that smell?' Sarah called out as she came in through the front door.

'Just a joss stick that went a bit out of control,' I replied as Gabe's words curled up and burned in a small, chipped china bowl.

Chapter Twenty-Nine

I had to get out of the house. Sarah had come back from work and gone straight into the kitchen to experiment with recipes for the Soul Food wraps that she was going to sell at the festival. I had no direction in mind, I just kept on walking.

I stumbled down the lane and across the field. I didn't take in the scenery – I was too preoccupied with Gabe's letter. When I did look up I saw Gabe everywhere. Leaning against the stone fence looking up at me and smiling or pacing around a tree trunk. To me he was as much a part of the Netherby landscape as the trees and grass.

Why did this HIV virus have to be in Gabe in the first place? Why did it have to be his mum that received the contaminated blood transfusion? Could Gabe ever have children? I thought about all the portraits of his family stretching back generations. Would it all end with him?

There was a chance that Gabe wouldn't be around in a few years' time and we would have wasted so much precious time.

If he were ill with something else, I could bear it. The whole community could bear it. They'd hold fundraisers and bake him cakes, go on sponsored walks to raise money for research. Pop stars would sing at a benefit concert for him, but if they knew he had HIV, the community would gossip and be afraid and warn their children to keep away from him. They'd be embarrassed and awkward around him.

It started to rain, but I didn't care. Actually, I was pleased. It matched my mood. The world was a shitty place. Let it rain. I didn't button up my jacket – instead I let the rain soak me.

At first I thought there was something wrong with me. Something missing. I couldn't even cry. But now I realise that crying was about letting go, and if I let go I would have to admit that I was crying for myself as well as for Gabe – and crying for all those things that we might never have and that everyone else took for granted.

Anyway, what was the point of crying when no amount of tears would change the situation?

The rain began to fall heavily, forcing me to take shelter under a tree. For a long while I stayed under the tree, letting the drips of rain fall on my face.

But it was one of those days when it was sunny and rainy at the same time. The rays of sunlight lit up the drops of rain. A wood pigeon flew up into the tree and began rustling above my head, shaking more of the raindrops down on my head. Then, as quickly as it had begun, the rain stopped and the sun took over. The air smelled fresh and clean. Some birds began to sing. I noticed a small clump of delicate pale blue flowers close to my feet. It was as if they had been refreshed by the rain shower.

I was totally aware of the beauty of this moment.

For the first time since Gabe had told me his news, I began to think clearly.

What was I doing? What good would pacing the country-side like an extra from a film version of *Wuthering Heights* do me or him?

I had to be strong for Gabriel. He had trusted me and expected nothing of me in return other than that I keep his secret. He had prepared himself for rejection and given me a free pass out of the relationship. Hadn't he told me in his letter that he was prepared to forget about me?

Something shifted inside me. Why had I been stressing about Mia and Jackson? Like Gabe said, they didn't care about me. All they cared about was causing trouble and then wheedling out of the consequences. I had acted so weak. So desperate for their friendship that I had simply accepted the situation as they dictated it.

Now I had an even bigger secret to keep. Was I up to it? Could I keep it even from my mum? It would help to talk about Gabe with somebody who understood about HIV.

My jacket began to steam as the heat from the sun mixed with the rain-drenched fabric. I turned and walked across the field. I had no idea what time it was, but I decided to head for the village and whatever company I could find there.

I was marching up the high street when I saw her glaring out of the café window at me. A slanging match with Cleo was the last thing I needed right now so I dropped my head and walked on by.

I had just made it a few paces past the café when she called my name.

'Look, I'm in no mood for a . . .' I began, and then I looked at her expression and stopped myself. She didn't look angry.

'Come round to the back. I need to talk to you.' She pointed to a little alleyway at the side of the shop.

Still a little wary of Cleo's unpredictability, I followed her round the corner and up to a brightly painted door.

Cleo pulled out a key. 'Come inside for a bit. You're soaked.'

'Got caught in the rain,' I replied lightly.

Cleo's flat was small but cosy. She threw me a towel and I began to rub at my hair.

'I'll make you some tea.' She went into the tiny kitchen.

'Won't they miss you in the café?'

'I'm on a break. Besides, we need to talk.'

She returned moments later and placed two large mugs down on the table.

The tea was too hot to drink so I blew on it to keep myself busy. I didn't want to talk right now.

Cleo settled herself on the sofa. 'Gabe told me about the letter.'

I looked up warily. Was this some kind of a test?

I nodded.

'I know everything about Gabe,' she said.

I nodded again. Why did I feel that she was out to trap me? Would I always feel this overwhelming fear of giving away his secret whenever Gabe came up in conversation?

'For some crazy reason he has decided to trust you.'

I stood up. 'It's time I went.'

'I'm sorry, Jenna. If Gabriel has been honest with you, then I need to tell you something. Gabriel and I have this really close bond.'

'He's told me about it and so have you.' I didn't want her trying to make me jealous again.

'I know for a fact that he wouldn't tell you everything.'

'I know that you went out with each other for a while.' As I said it, I was struck by a horrible thought. What if Gabe had infected Cleo?

'I am HIV-positive too.'

It was like somebody had pulled the plug on my brain and I slumped to the floor.

'How long have I been out?' I asked when I came round. Cleo had put a pillow under my head and covered me with a blanket.

She smiled. 'I thought you'd be surprised, but I didn't think you'd pass out on me.'

I sat up. Cleo pulled another cushion off the sofa and sat down next to me.

'Look, Jenna. I don't like you that much, but if Gabe has chosen to put his trust in you then I will have to as well. But if you mess him about or hurt him in any way I'll see that you pay for it. If it's the last thing I ever do.'

She fixed me with a hard stare. I was left in no doubt that she meant what she said.

'We met when I was eleven and Gabe was nine. We met in hospital. We were both beginning to guess the truth about those bugs in the blood – that we might have the same illness as our mums.'

Gabe had told me that both of them had lost a mother. He hadn't told me it was from the same cause, though.

'Gabe saved my life. He keeps my spirits up. We look out for each other. We know how the other is feeling without saying anything. He is feeling pretty upset at the moment about you.'

I swallowed. There was a huge lump in my throat. Cleo and I would never be best buddies, but maybe we could learn to get along.

'How are you feeling?' Cleo wiped a hair out of my face.

'Like I'm living in a parallel universe that looks like earth, but nothing is quite the same.'

Cleo smiled again. 'Most of the time I feel like the keeper of a deep, dark secret. I watch everyone. Trust no one. School is a nightmare. Never daring to tell anyone. Having to listen to all their ignorant comments about people with AIDS and not being able to say a thing in case it drew attention to me. One time I made the mistake of pointing out that being HIV-positive wasn't the same as having AIDS. Someone then piped up, "How come you know so much?" and the spotlight landed straight on me . . . You feel so isolated. Mum couldn't really believe it was that bad because when she was at school it was during the height of AIDS awareness. It was still a new discovery and they were giving lots of information. My school didn't tell us much on account of it being a strict church school. Nowadays it's up to each school what they decide to teach you about in sex education. So I learned to shut up and say nothing, even when people came out with the most outrageous things.'

'It sounds awful.'

'Welcome to my world, Jenna. There's only one place that kept me sane and that was a special youth club in London that Gabe and I go to. It's the one place where we can truly be ourselves and not feel judged.'

I thought back to what Gabe had said in his letter about being able to relax when he was with me. I felt a buzz. It made me feel special.

'I won't do anything to hurt Gabe,' I said.

'You'd better not.' Cleo's eyes burned fiercely. 'Gabe and I have been through a lot together. I'd better be getting back to work. Break time's over. See you later on tonight at the rehearsal. And don't tell *anyone*!'

'I won't,' I said.

Chapter Thirty

t was now late afternoon and the high street had filled up with people, talking about the festival or carrying boxes of food. Out of the corner of my eye I saw someone that I thought was Mia, but it turned out to be a false alarm. Meeting up with her right now was the last thing I needed.

I was actually looking forward to doing some work in the shop. There were hours to go before the rehearsal and I needed some distraction. Finding out first about Gabe and then Cleo was too mind-blowing. It made me wonder how many other HIV-positive kids there were out there and what sort of a time they were having. I also realised how little I really knew about it.

I had so many questions. What was the difference between HIV and AIDS? Cleo had said they were different. What would happen if Gabe cut himself and I touched some of the blood? I knew that kissing him was probably fine, but would he ever be able to make love?

I felt shallow for being so jealous of Gabe and Cleo's friendship. There were parts of Gabe's life that only Cleo could really understand, and I would always be an onlooker. No wonder Gabe had laughed at the stupid mess I'd got myself into with Mia and Jackson. Bet he'd trade my problems for his any day.

As I walked into the shop, I was feeling less afraid. 'I can and I *will* deal with it,' I told myself.

I know Gabe would never do anything to put me in danger. I had to stop thinking of myself. Where was he now? How was he feeling? I wished that I could push the hair out of his face and squeeze his fingers to let him know that everything was all right. I wouldn't walk away from this relationship.

As I breezed into the shop Julius frowned at me and raised his eyebrows in a warning signal which I was just trying to figure out when I noticed the vase on the counter and behind it sat Sarah frowning and chewing her nails.

'So you found it,' I said.

Sarah flared up at me, 'Is that all you can say? Well, at least you're not pretending to act surprised.'

'No,' I began. 'I was going to tell you, but something came up.'

Sarah shook her head and yelled. 'You are incredible! How you can just stand there so cool after this. You knew how much this vase meant to me.'

I raised my voice to match hers. 'I'm sorry. I should have told you sooner.'

'Why did you do it, Jenna? After all I've done for you. You just don't seem to care. Did it give you some kind of buzz? I would have given you as much money as I could spare –'

'Aunt Sarah, stop! I didn't take your bloody vase! I only saw your vase in the shop window yesterday and I was going to tell you about it. I was pretty certain it was the same vase. I mean, there can't be that many hideous-patterned vases in the area.'

'DON'T MAKE JOKES AT A TIME LIKE THIS!' Sarah screamed at me.

'Think I'll pop out for a breath of fresh air,' said Julius, edging his way out towards the door.

'STAY!' Sarah commanded. Julius froze. Sarah turned back to me. Her face was white with rage.

'Julius is going to drive us over to the shop and you are going to apologise to Angie, the owner of the shop, for selling her a vase that didn't belong to you. It was her assistant who bought the vase and she is working there this afternoon. Lucy will ID you and then Angie may want to call the police and I certainly won't stop her. Angie does not want word going around that her shop receives stolen goods. It's about time you started facing up to the consequences of your actions.'

'Why are you so sure it's me?' I fumed.

'Lucy says she bought the vase off a young girl with long brown hair and a London accent.' Sarah was putting on her jacket. 'I'm not going to push it all under the carpet like my sister. This time you are going to face the truth of the situation.'

The angry part of me gritted my teeth and followed them out of the shop.

'Fine,' I said. I knew it wasn't going to be me who was going to get hurt in the long run. So, Kai was sending his new girlfriend on all his dirty little errands. She had been sent to check that his precious record collection was safe and sell Sarah's stuff to the antique shop.

In the car I mellowed a bit. 'Sarah, please believe that it wasn't me.'

She turned the car radio on to drown out my plea.

I tried again outside the shop. 'We don't have to do this,' I said.

Sarah ignored me and marched into the shop. For a split second I thought about going along with it and saying I took the vase, to stop her from finding out the painful truth this way.

'Facing the truth is not all it's cracked up to be,' I muttered as I followed her into the shop.

Angie was a tall, smartly dressed woman. She and Sarah kissed each other on both cheeks. Angie tutted sympathetically at Sarah whilst at the same time throwing me a dirty look.

From the back of the shop a door opened and a girl came out carrying a heavy tea tray. Lucy looked me up and down. 'She's got the same length of hair, but the girl I bought the vase off had dark brown hair, not reddish.'

'Are you sure? Hair colour can change in the light,' Angie insisted. I got the feeling that she was disappointed that it wasn't me.

Angie poured some tea. Lucy handed me a delicate china cup and looked at me again and said, 'Oh I forgot. There was a man waiting outside for her in a car. He had long curly black hair. Looked a bit like an old rock star.'

Sarah winced as if she'd been kicked and then she quickly recovered.

'Kai must have taken it and forgotten to let me know.' She swallowed her hot tea down quickly and went to leave.

Angie scowled at Lucy. 'You never mentioned that there was a man with her before.'

'You never asked me,' Lucy answered, sticking her chin out defiantly. I got the feeling that Lucy was not happy in her work.

Sarah laughed it off. 'It's probably one of his madcap schemes. It usually means he's creating some new poetry.'

I glared. As we were walking to the door I turned, looked at everyone and said, 'I accept your humble apologies.'

Lucy giggled and said, 'No way it could have been you. The girl who came in the shop was pregnant. Oops! I must have "forgotten" to mention that too!'

Chapter Thirty-One

So much for the peace and quiet of the countryside that everyone raved about. This place was full of surprises. Living in London was like a rest cure compared to this. I wondered how Jackson and Mia would find it.

I really wished that they weren't coming. I was in no mood to listen to them poking fun at everyone and everything in sight. Maybe Rebecca's brother would be flaky and pull out at the last minute.

This time Sarah didn't take to her bed and weep. I wished she would cry or get mad or say something, but she just sat stony-faced in the front room. I couldn't begin to imagine what she must be feeling. She hadn't had children because Kai didn't want them. Now he was leaving her for a young woman who was going to have his baby. How hurtful is that? Plus he was stealing from her. I felt my jaw tightening and my hand curling into a fist at the mere thought of him.

Even Tallulah was spooked. She ran about the house in a demented way.

The rain had cleared and the sun was setting, leaving a pale raspberry ripple of light in the sky. The vase episode had taken my mind off things for a while, but it was getting close to the time of the rehearsal. I wondered what the others would say if

Gabe wasn't there and whether I'd have to give an explanation, or would Cleo do it?

I cleared away Sarah's untouched mug of tea and poured her a new one.

'The rehearsal won't last too long. I'll bring you back some chips. Will you be all right?'

Sarah nodded slowly. It was a relief to be leaving the house for a while.

Charlie and Freddie were already unloading the van when I arrived at the shop.

Freddie grinned. 'Jenna, the last of the posse . . . er . . . what I mean is, that you are the last person to arrive. Not to worry because Julius let us in.'

Charlie rolled his eyes. 'I'm not sure which is worse – hip-hop slang or endless sentences. We're going to start in a few minutes.'

I glanced round the shop. 'Is everyone here?'

He nodded. So Gabe had made it back from his meeting in London after all.

'Cleo is getting changed. Gabe is just helping Julius with the camera equipment. We've been asked to supply some photos.'

'And Julius is going to take them?' I asked as I prepared myself to face Gabe. I wasn't sure how to act. If I played it too cool, he'd think it was over between us, and if I was too friendly, then the others would catch on.

Charlie came closer. 'You OK, Jenna? You don't mind Julius taking some pictures, do you? He was massive in the old days. Used to photograph rock stars and models.'

'Why am I not surprised?' I muttered, looking down at my crumpled jeans and the food stain on the side of my T-shirt. If I acted all put out then it would mask my reactions to seeing

Gabe again. 'I'm dressed for a rehearsal not a photo session,' I grumbled. Let people think I'm vain and trivial.

Cleo made an entrance wearing a tight black dress, small black cowboy hat and silver chain around her neck. She looked stunning.

'You look fine,' Gabe said in a quiet voice that made me jump. Then he added, whispering now, 'I came back from London early. Did what I had to do and decided that I had to carry on with my life.'

Cleo was in a manic mood and she seemed determined to monopolise Gabe's attention. For once I didn't mind. Gabe and Cleo needed each other.

But as I was swigging from a bottle of water he stood beside me and whispered, 'Have you read my letter?'

I nodded.

'Let's meet up tonight, usual place but an hour later.'

I nodded again. I was about to reach out and touch him, but he deliberately moved away. Then everything got crazy for a while as Julius set up his equipment.

'Just act natural,' he said as he switched on a bright spotlight and dazzled us all.

Cleo grabbed hold of Gabe, Freddie struck mean poses, Charlie looked startled and I tried to melt into the background.

Behind a camera Julius transformed himself into a camp monster screeching weird stuff at us from 'Fromage, my lovelies, say fromage!' to 'Love the camera, love the camera – now hate the camera, hate the camera.'

Ava came in the shop dressed to the nines in a sparkly top and freshly applied make-up. She put on a pathetic charade of acting surprised that we were having our photographs taken and being reluctant to join us.

There was just enough time to run through the order of the songs and make a half-hearted attempt at playing them. We'd used up all our energy posing.

As we were packing up, Charlie handed out our performers' passes to the festival. They were plastic bracelets.

'Don't lose these or you'll never get in,' he said. 'Plus, we've been allocated a corner in the performers' area, close to the stage, where we can camp and use as a space to store our clothes and instruments.'

'I don't have a tent,' I said.

'The vicar is lending us one of the cub scout tents for us all to sleep in,' said Freddie. 'So that all the groupies and free-loaders can come and party after the show. We are playing on Saturday so we can spend Friday settling in and listening to the other bands or whatever.'

'In your dreams, Freddie. We're not sharing a tent with the likes of you – are we, Gabe?' Cleo asked.

But Gabe wasn't listening. He looked down at his watch, threw on his coat and walked out of the door. This time, he at least managed a short wave goodbye. Cleo followed him out of the door.

Charlie sighed. 'I'm the lead singer so it should be me who's the mean and moody one.'

I ruffled his hair. 'Come on, let's go for some chips.'

Now I could understand Gabe's moods.

Charlie and I walked back home together, stopping on the way to buy the chips I promised Sarah. Charlie was unusually quiet, and I wasn't saying much either. I supposed he was getting nervous about playing at the festival and my head was in a spin thinking about Gabe and what we would say to each other. Half of me was excited and the other half was scared that I'd stuff up. Charlie sighed and threw half his chips in a bin.

I said, 'You know what they say in the theatre – bad dress rehearsal, great show!'

Charlie grinned. 'It's been really great having you sing with the band. Maybe we could go out together when we're both back in London?'

I was startled. Was Charlie asking me out? Charlie noticed and backtracked. 'When I said go out, I meant to listen to some more anti-folk bands so you can see what they are like. Maybe eat some more pizza afterwards.'

'That would be great,' I said. I didn't want to hurt his feelings so I said, 'I hope we'll go out lots, Charlie. You've been a good friend to me in Netherby and I'd like it to continue.'

He walked quickly inside.

Sarah was still sitting in the front room.

'I brought you some chips,' I said as I unwrapped the package. I had also bought a fish cake for Tallulah that I crumbled into her dish.

'I'm not hungry,' Sarah said slowly.

In desperation, I began to babble on about the photo shoot, the rehearsal – anything I could think of to cut into the awful silence in the room.

'Have you got the food stall ready? I could give you a hand. And the poetry tombola?'

Sarah sat up bolt upright and said, 'Kai will be at the festival and then we can sort out this misunderstanding. Must get everything ready. No time to lose.' Then she began to manically pace about the room. I'm not sure which was worse. This frantic activity or when she never moved a muscle.

I went upstairs to pack my stuff for the festival. I hadn't

really given much thought to what I was going to wear on stage. I'm sure Cleo had, though. She had seemed really wired tonight and even more focused on Gabe than usual. I put on my Walkman and played my CDs as loud as I could to blot out the frantic bustling and rustling noises from downstairs.

There I was, only a few weeks ago, thinking I was so grown up because Mia was my best friend and Jackson liked me; and how cool it was to keep them out of trouble and lose my place at school because of it. Now all that felt like childish stuff. Gabe was right to laugh at me.

Then it hit me just how much I needed Gabe. How much I valued his presence in my life. How many different sides of me he could see. I thought of all the 'Our Times' we had spent together. For a brief time I had stopped thinking about him as a person and let some germ in his body affect the way I felt about him! There was so much more to him than that. When I saw him later tonight I was going to let him know how much he meant to me.

I crept downstairs to check on Sarah before I left. As I switched off my music I could hear manic laughing. My first thought was that Sarah had completely lost it, but then I heard some familiar voices.

'*Mum!*' I screeched. I'd never been so pleased to see her. Even Marcus was there.

'You dark horse, Jenna. Once I found out that you were performing at the Netherby Festival I had to come.'

'You'll never get tickets. They sold out ages ago,' I said.

'Lucky for us that Sarah sent me some.'

'I always send your mum a ticket for sentimental reasons,' Sarah said with a sigh.

'We went to the first ever Netherby Festival when we were teenagers,' Mum explained.

'We both fell in love with the same boy,' Sarah added, giggling.

Mum laughed. 'We trailed him round a field for hours on end.'

'Scary thought,' I said as Marcus jumped up and down on the sofa, screeching, 'Did you kiss him? Did you kiss him?'

'That'd be telling,' Mum said with a wink.

'*Please* don't do that,' I said darkly.

'Marcus, you can help me run the poetry tombola,' Sarah said. She was looking more like her normal self.

Marcus frowned. 'What's that? It sounds weird.'

'It's great fun. People pay money for a ticket and if they pull out a raffle ticket that ends in zero or five, then they win one of my poems.'

'Can I keep some of the money?' Marcus asked.

'No way,' said Mum.

'I'll pay you a fee for managing the stall,' Sarah said.

'I want paying in money, not poems,' Marcus said and we all laughed.

'So my dark horse of a daughter is now a backing singer in a band.' Mum sat next to me on the sofa and patted my knee.

'Not just backing. I'm going to sing a song too – "Because the Night!"'

'My favourite song!' Mum exclaimed.

'I'm doing an anti-folk version,' I explained.

'Oh, I see,' she said, clearly not seeing at all.

'It's an alternative music to manufactured pop music. Apart from my song, everything else has been written by the band.'

Mum jumped up and asked, 'Sarah, is that old trunk of mine still in the box room?'

'I think so . . .' Sarah said, frowning. I guess she couldn't be sure what else Kai had taken a fancy to.

Mum dragged me upstairs while Sarah and Marcus made hot chocolate. She pulled out a dusty old trunk from underneath a pile of cardboard boxes in the box room.

As soon as we were on our own she said, 'Spill.'

I shook my head, but inside I was panicking. What did she know?

But I was just being paranoid. Of course Mum didn't know anything about Gabe. Is this how keeping other people's secrets made you?

'Let me remind you, my little clam of a daughter, that Sarah is my sister. She looks terrible. What has Kai done this time?'

It was a relief to be able to tell Mum something about what had been bothering me. I left out the bit about Sarah accusing me of stealing the vase, but I kept in the bit about Kai's pregnant girlfriend.

Mum didn't say much, but I could see by the tightness around her mouth that she was cross.

'Aha. Here it is.' She pulled out a crackly cellophane-wrapped parcel. She handed it to me.

Inside it was a T-shirt. The cotton was thin and on the front was a faded screen print of Patti Smith.

'I bought it from a second-hand clothing stand in Camden Market about twenty years ago. It comes from her first concert in London in the 1970s. You can wear it.'

It was perfect! 'Thanks, Mum.'

Gabe would love it, I thought. Then suddenly I glanced at

the clock. It was already twenty past ten. It would take me at least another ten minutes to race to the treehouse. Would Gabe wait for me?

'Forgot something for the concert!' I yelled as I ran down the stairs two at a time.

I was out of the door before anyone could stop me.

Chapter Thirty-Two

Too late. By the time I'd made it to the treehouse, there was no sign of Gabe.

'You could have given me a chance and waited!' I yelled to the empty space.

When I got back I noticed that there was a scrap of paper with a stone holding it down on the wall opposite the cottage, where Gabe liked to sit. It was a page torn out of his astronomy notebook. On the blank page he had written:

> *I understand, and you're probably right ending things now. It's too difficult for us to be together.*
> *Thanks for what we had.*
> *Love, Gabe*

I started back down the hill. I had to catch up with Gabe and explain that I was only late because Mum had showed up and that I wasn't brushing him off.

I made it as close as I could to Netherby Hall, but the road leading up to the house was fenced off and a group of menacing security guards stood outside. The festival had transformed the quiet countryside into a bustling city.

I turned back to walk down the hill past a stream of parked cars queuing to get into the festival site. I had to let Gabe know that he was wrong about me. There would be no time to talk once we were caught up with the band stuff at the festival. The church bell sounded eleven times. I had to find him soon!

As I was making my way down past the stream of traffic, the window of a battered old car wound down and a voice shouted, 'Jenna!'

Oh no! I thought. Could this evening get any worse?

In the car were Mia, Jackson and Rebecca.

Mia shrieked, 'We made it! It's taken us hours to drive down.'

Rebecca said, 'The car broke down and we had to wait ages for the AA.'

Jackson reached out his hand and touched my arm. 'Good to see you, Jenna. Thanks for the e-mail.'

Rebecca looked a bit peeved, but said, 'We heard you got a job working on a food stall. That sounds like fun.' Although she said it in a way that really meant, 'I'd rather have all of my teeth pulled out by a pair of pliers.'

I couldn't be bothered telling them that I was also performing at the festival. Let them find out that for themselves, the snobs!

'Have you found another school yet?' Rebecca wasn't letting go of that knife she was digging into me just yet.

Jackson looked suitably embarrassed and Mia looked away.

Rebecca's brother, Justin, piped up from the driver's seat, 'So *this* is the girl. The one who went shopping with a teacher's credit card? Cool.'

'We're looking forward to meeting Charlie,' Mia said and winked.

'Charlie's just a friend,' I snapped back. Mia had this way of getting under my skin and making me feel vulnerable. I used to accept it, but now they all seemed so insignificant. I wasn't going to let her take control of me any more.

Jackson smiled. He was the only one who really looked genuinely pleased to see me.

'We'll see you in there,' Mia said, waving to me as the line of traffic began to move again.

'Not if I see you first,' I said. Everyone laughed, but I meant it. Meeting up with them again made me feel awkward and a little sad. It was like their friendship was a pair of party shoes that I'd grown out of.

Mum had been too busy trying to prise information out of Sarah to notice how late it was when I got home. She even lent me her mobile so I could ring Netherby Hall. I'd made up some excuse about needing to finalise an urgent arrangement. It was constantly engaged.

My head was spinning. Gabe thought I didn't want to be with him. He must think I'm really shallow and trivial to give up on him so easily. And Cleo would be only too pleased to back up that idea.

Mum was too preoccupied with Sarah to see how messed up I was. Besides, she'd surely put any restlessness on my part down to the fact that I was performing tomorrow.

As I crept up to bed the church bell rang for midnight. I felt my insides tighten. Everything felt hopeless.

Marcus was curled up on a mattress on the floor in my room. He couldn't sleep either.

'We missed you in Florida,' he said. 'Mum cried, you know, because she felt so bad that you weren't there.'

'I missed you too,' I said. 'But those postcards you sent me made me feel as if I was there.'

'Is that a love letter you've got in your hand?' he asked me, teasingly.

I'd forgotten that I was still holding on to Gabe's note. 'I suppose it is,' I whispered.

I closed my eyes and tried to sleep. I would sort things out as soon as I could tomorrow.

We all had to get up early the next morning, because Sarah had begun cooking her Soul Food wraps. She seemed in much better spirits. I think she and Mum had been up half the night talking. Marcus was painting a sign for the poetry tombola.

'Take lots of warm clothes. It gets cold at night in a tent,' Mum fussed.

'Not if you're sharing with three sweaty boys and a girl,' I said.

Mum raised an eyebrow and said, 'I don't know if I'm totally comfortable with that . . .'

But Sarah said, 'We shared a tent with six boys once, remember? That was all perfectly innocent.'

Mum sighed. 'I suppose there is safety in numbers . . .'

'These boys are really nice,' said Sarah. 'One of them is Lord Netherby's son.'

'Cleo will be there as well,' I snorted. 'She can keep an eye on me.'

Mum raised another eyebrow. I comforted myself slightly with the knowledge that at least I'd be seeing Gabe today.

'I think it's Charlie who has got the key to Jenna's heart,' Sarah said, smiling.

The rest of us pretended to stick fingers down our throats.

'We all just get along as mates,' I insisted.

'But it's obvious both Charlie and Freddie are besotted

with you,' Sarah continued, biting on a piece of toast.

'Obvious to whom?' I said.

'Anyone who's got a pair of eyes. The only one who isn't interested in you is Gabriel.'

'You are so wise,' I said. 'How do you do it?'

'My poetic intuition,' Sarah said with a grin.

Chapter Thirty-Three

The plastic bracelets that Charlie had given us worked like a charm. I was given instant access to the site. I was desperate to see Gabe. As he didn't have a mobile I tried the Netherby Hall phone again this morning, but his line was still engaged. It seemed that the whole world wanted to speak to Lord Netherby about the festival.

All paths leading to Netherby Hall were now sealed off with metal fences, and patrolled by mean-looking security guards in black bomber jackets.

It was shaping up to be another hot day. The sky was bright blue and there were no clouds. All the fields were filling up with tents. The sound of builders yelling and swearing filled the air as the main stage was erected.

I should have been feeling excited to be a part of it all, but instead I felt tiny and small and hurt. It felt like everything was working against Gabe and me. He had probably convinced himself by now that I was finished with him. He had been so sure that I would leave him.

'Of all the fields in the world and you had to walk into mine! Hello there, old chum!'

'Julius!' I was so pleased to see a familiar face.

'I spotted you standing amidst this flotsam and jetsam.' He

nodded at the groups of campers that were already coming into this field. 'I've got the photos. Pulled a few strings with the wedding photographer in Greater Netherby and he let me use his dark room last night.'

He handed me a brown envelope. Inside it was a wodge of black-and-white photographs.

'Haven't lost my touch, have I?'

'They are brilliant,' I gasped. There was one picture in particular that caught my eye. I was standing at one end of the counter, Charlie and Ava were dancing in the centre, Freddie was posing and Cleo was draped around Gabe. Funny thing was he was looking up at me and I was looking back at him.

Julius cleared his throat. 'They say a picture says more than a thousand words.'

I slipped the photo back in the envelope.

'I am an old fool who has wasted many a year walking the primrose path of dalliance, but I do believe in love,' Julius said.

I half-expected him to come out with one of his silly jokes or bad puns, but for once he didn't. He just said, 'I'm off to deliver these to the publicity office – otherwise known as the kitchen at Netherby Hall.'

'Could you do me a big favour?' I asked.

Julius nodded.

'Tell Gabe that I need to see him, right away.'

'Your word is my command.' Julius bowed and I hugged him.

I sat down underneath a large tree on the edge of the field to wait.

The sun moved higher in the sky. I could feel its heat on my face. I closed my eyes and rewrote life for a while.

In my first daydream, Ms Rose had taken her credit card with her that day. We had all got caught messing about in her office and were sent to the head's office where Mia was so rude to the headteacher that she got expelled and was dragged kicking and screaming from the school.

My second daydream involved a discovery of a pill that killed the HIV virus. This was followed by a fantastic dream about the huge success of Goats in a Spin. I pictured thousands of Julius's photos on posters plastered all over London. There would be rave reviews in all the indie music magazines.

'Jenna?'

I half-opened my eyes as Jackson sat down beside me.

'How you doing?' he asked.

'How did you manage to find me?' There must have been thousands of people around the place.

He smiled at me. 'You stand out in a crowd, Jenna.'

Jackson had lost none of his charm over the summer break.

I laughed, then sat up and looked around me in an exaggerated way.

'Where's your fan club? Or are they your minders?' I asked.

He chuckled softly. 'That's what I like about you, Jenna. You've got a great sense of humour as well as being gorgeous.' He looked at me out of the corner of his eye.

I fanned the air. 'Phew, it's so hot already and it's not even midday.'

'Look, Jenna. I'm really sorry about what happened. I think it's great that you haven't grassed us up. You know I'd do the same for you if the circumstances were the other way around.'

I shook my head as my lips formed a tight smile. 'Here's your big opportunity, Jackson. When you stop and think about it, "the circumstances" are the other way around. I'm taking all the blame. My reputation is in tatters and you could rescue me with a few simple words.'

He looked at me with his deep, big brown eyes of his that for a second I wished I still loved him. I remembered how I'd felt after he had first kissed me. I recalled all the fun we'd had messing around, playing silly games and having a laugh. Jackson was fun to be with. If I were back with Jackson things could go back to the way they were. My life would be so much easier if I still loved him and not Gabe.

Then I reminded myself about all the other times that had not been so good and I said, 'Thing is, Jackson. If the roles had been reversed, I wouldn't have expected you to take all the blame. That wouldn't be right. I would have been scared witless, but I would have owned up. My conscience would've made me.'

Jackson moved closer. I took a deep breath. He was as handsome as ever.

'Things aren't always that clear cut, Jenna. I'd had a few problems at my other school. Got myself a bit of a reputation. The slightest whiff of trouble and my mum'll pack me off to school in Nigeria.'

'If we had all stood together and explained, then maybe not. I'm sure your mum values honesty. Besides, didn't you and Mia promise to come clean when the time was right?'

Jackson nodded.

'Trouble is the time will never be right, will it?'

Jackson shook his head and sucked his teeth. 'Jenna, will you stop giving me a hard time? Things haven't turned out too badly, have they?'

I thought about my life in Netherby – Gabe, the band and the job in the bookshop . . . and I smiled.

'Better than I could have imagined, actually.'

'Well then, let's kiss and make up. No hard feelings?' He put his arms around me and nuzzled in my hair.

At first I pulled back, but Jackson only laughed and pulled me closer.

What could be the harm in sharing one uncomplicated farewell kiss?

Chapter Thirty-Four

'm not sure exactly how long Gabe had been standing there, but judging from the expression on his face it was long enough to jump to the wrong conclusion.

'Julius said you wanted to see me,' he said. 'But I really should be going. Charlie needs a hand with the tent. Is this your *friend* from London?'

I didn't like the way he put the emphasis on friend. Like it meant more than that.

'This is Jackson. He's come with Mia and some mates,' I said.

I turned to Jackson. 'This is Gabe. We're in a band together. We're performing in the Fringe Tent tomorrow.'

Jackson looked surprised. 'My girl is in a band. Jenna, you are full of surprises.' He hugged me again.

'I'm not your girl,' I snarled, and pulled away from him, but it was too late. Gabe was already walking the other way back across the field.

Jackson laughed and reached for me again, but this time I stood well back. I had to keep my distance from him, because letting him get close was dangerous. The look on Gabe's face had proved that. Now I had even more explaining to do. What had I been thinking of letting him anywhere near me?

In the distance I could see Aurora racing towards us, waving her arms in the air. She caught up with Gabe first and then he turned round and pointed in my direction. Gabe stayed put and Aurora kept running towards me.

Between gasps she said, 'Jenna, come quick! Sarah needs help! Come on.'

Although I didn't ask him to, Jackson came along as well.

Aurora pulled on Gabe's arm as she ran past him.

My first thought was that Kai had shown up and things had got ugly. But when I got there, everyone was standing around a large tree, looking up. Marcus was holding his jumper open under the tree.

'It's Tallulah. She followed us here, got frightened by the crowds and ran up the tree in a panic.'

Sure enough, at the top of a large oak tree – and perched on a branch too thin for her fat body – sat Tallulah.

'We've got to get her down before something awful happens to her!' Sarah wailed.

'What goes up by itself must come down,' Jackson said with a laugh.

'Your boyfriend's got a point,' said Gabe churlishly.

I sighed helplessly. Gabe should have more faith in me and not expect the worst. After all, I trusted him and coped with watching Cleo draped all over him at every chance she got. He shouldn't have been so quick to jump to conclusions when he saw Jackson and me. *And* he should have waited for me at the treehouse the other night. Now we are both hurting.

Something inside me snapped. I launched myself into action.

'Why is everyone just standing around? I'm going up to get her.'

'I'll be your ground back-up, Jenna,' Marcus said as he stretched his jumper out even further.

'I'll help.' Aurora unbuttoned her cardigan and stood beside Marcus.

Jackson just laughed again and said, 'This is crazy, man.'

But I wasn't listening. I was climbing and trying to blot out that voice in my head that kept asking, 'So, what are you going to do now?' as I wobbled my way up the tree towards Tallulah.

I missed my footing a couple of times and snapped a few branches on the way, but at least I was leaving the ground and my problems behind me for a while.

If I had any idea that Tallulah would be grateful for this act of heroism I was wrong. The first thing she did was hiss and lash out at me with her claws. Then she wriggled like she was about to take a flying leap.

'Cats are not suicidal,' I reassured myself and I began to talk to her in that pathetic itsy-bitsy voice that Sarah always used with her.

It seemed to calm her down for a while. She backed off to the thicker end of the branch and closed her eyes. I tried to ignore the stinging on my arm where she'd scratched me.

'Just keep talking to her,' Gabe said. To my surprise, he was following me up the tree on the other side and was positioned behind Tallulah.

'Gabe, I have no idea what to do next. I'm scared,' I hissed at him.

He smiled. 'So am I, but we have to look as if we know what we're doing. Can't let our audience down.'

I swallowed, looked down at the others and tried to calm the dizzy feeling in my stomach.

A crowd had formed and now I became aware of a babble of voices I recognised. I could make out Charlie, Freddie and Mia.

'I think I'm going to be sick,' I said.

'You'll be fine.'

'What if I've just made things worse? What if I end up frightening Tallulah into jumping? This is such a bad idea.'

'Just deal with it, Jenna. There's no time to be afraid,' Gabe said fiercely as he began to take off his T-shirt.

'I don't think doing a strip will help,' I said, trying to focus on that familiar torso to calm my nerves.

Gabe ignored me and said in a serious tone, 'I'm going to count to three, then I'm going to grab her from behind, wrap the T-shirt around her to disable her claws. You keep talking to her.'

I put on that soppy voice again. 'Who's a silly sod of a mangy old pussy cat, then? Getting yourself wedged up a tree.'

Gabe lunged at her with the shirt. After an initial struggle she settled down and allowed herself to be tucked up in the T-shirt. Gabe balanced her under one arm and climbed down.

They both looked up at me. Tallulah blinked and Gabe said, 'Jenna, you can do it.'

He didn't give me chance to respond as he moved further down the tree. All those feelings of fear for Tallulah and anger at the world in general had evaporated. Another chance to be alone with Gabe had been missed. Now I was just a wobbly jelly, stuck up a tree afraid for myself, with a large audience watching my humiliation.

I heard Mia saying, 'She'll never get down by herself,' followed by Rebecca's giggles.

That spurred me on. I slid down and landed with a back and knee-jarring thump on the ground below.

Mia ran over to hug me. 'That was so brave, girlfriend!' she cooed.

'Are you all right, Jenna?' Charlie asked, sounding genuinely concerned.

'I'm fine, Charlie,' I said. Gabe and the others were nowhere to be seen.

'You're crazy, risking your neck for a stupid cat,' Jackson said.

'Tallulah. What kind of weird name is that?' Rebecca added.

'Charlie! How nice to meet you. Jenna has told me all about you,' Mia exclaimed, fluttering her eyelashes at a bemused Charlie.

'Have you got something in your eye?' he asked her, pulling out a grubby tissue from his pocket. 'If you have, I can help you out.'

I spotted Mum standing behind them.

'Where's Tallulah?' I asked.

'Sarah and Aurora have taken her over to the house, Gabe thinks they've got a cat basket somewhere.'

I suddenly remembered Curio, her little cat that lived in the treehouse. What had happened to him?

Mum took me by the arm and led me away from the others.

After she'd checked me over, she frowned and said, 'What were you thinking of, inviting Mia to the festival?'

'I didn't invite her, Mum!'

What was it about me that made everyone jump to the wrong conclusion?

Chapter Thirty-Five

I turned and ran across the field as quickly as possible. I had a real job on my hands to convince the security guards standing by the entrance to Netherby Hall to let me in.

'The hall is out of bounds,' one of them said as he crossed his arms in front of his massive torso.

'I'm with the group of people who just came in with the cat,' I insisted, showing them the scratches on my arm.

They phoned the hall and eventually I was allowed in.

Everyone was gathered round the kitchen table. On the far end of the table was the most elaborate cat basket I'd ever seen. It was like a miniature version of Netherby Hall made out of wicker. Tallulah meowed at me.

'Someone's landed on their paws,' I said.

'Jenna, you were so brave! Come and sit next to me.' Aurora pointed to a space next to her at the kitchen table. 'Are you injured like Gabe?'

Gabe was sitting at the other end of the table. He had changed his T-shirt and Isobel was bathing some scratches on his arms.

'This'll sting, Gabe.'

I looked at the disinfectant and winced. I knew that Gabe

couldn't risk getting an infection. I looked at Gabe, but he looked away.

Marcus was chatting away to everyone.

'I'm sure my jumper would've taken Tallulah's weight if she'd decided to jump,' he said.

'Why jump when you can be carried down?' I said, trying desperately to catch Gabe's eye. He seemed equally determined *not* to look at me. I had to do something. I had let too many chances to sort things out go by. I wasn't going to waste another one.

'Last night I was desperate to see Cassiopeia, but the sky was too cloudy. And I was a bit late. Mum and Marcus turned up out of the blue,' I said.

'I wouldn't have had you down as a star-gazer,' Isobel said, looking surprised.

'I've got interested this summer. Found some books in the shop,' I said. Gabe still wouldn't look at me.

'She came back with a love letter,' Marcus chipped in.

'That was astronomical notes, silly,' I said. Gabe still didn't look at me.

Aurora came over and put a large mug in front of me. 'Have some special hot chocolate. Brave people are allowed a mug.'

I sniffed it. 'Mmm . . . smells of oranges.' I took a sip.

'Mum put some booze in it,' Aurora said as she sat down next to me.

'Liqueur, Aurora, orange liqueur. Honestly, I don't know where she gets it from.' Isobel shook her head disapprovingly.

'From you, Mummy,' Aurora said in a sickly sweet voice.

'It tastes great,' I said as I sipped the drink.

Sarah frowned. 'I should be getting back to the stall.'

'I'll take Tallulah back home,' I said. I needed a break from this place. I had made my feelings for Gabe known and I wasn't sure how he'd react. Now that he had had time to think things over again he may already have changed his mind about me!

'Gabe can drive you. That'll save time. Then he can pick up some groceries on the way back. I feel so besieged here at the moment,' Isobel said.

Well, there was a chance to find out what he was thinking.

'We'll come too,' Aurora said, standing up and giving Marcus a nudge.

'No, you won't. You're giving an interview to that hideous children's TV programme,' said Isobel.

'Which TV programme?' Marcus asked.

'*Hard Cheese*,' Aurora replied.

'*You're* going to be interviewed by Kelly and Leroy?' Marcus's eyes nearly popped out of his head.

Aurora nodded. 'You can come with me if you like.'

Gabe was putting on his jacket and reaching for the car keys off an old hook.

'We'd better get a move on. The traffic will be crazy.'

I reached over for the basket. 'Wait – won't you need it for your cat?' I asked Aurora.

Isobel handed Gabe a shopping list. 'Aurora doesn't have a cat.'

Gabe meowed.

Oh my God. I nearly gasped out loud. There hadn't been a cat at all! How embarrassing is that?

I waited till we were in the car before I said anything.

'Of all the low-down things to do, I think pretending to be a cat is the worst.'

Gabe laughed. 'It was the *kindest* thing to do. No one likes to be overheard boohooing.'

'How patronising,' I said, sniffing.

'Besides, if you'd known that I'd seen you all bleary-eyed and crazy, then I wouldn't have stood a chance with you. First impressions are really important.'

'Actually, I remember very clearly the first time I saw you.'

'In the shop?'

I shook my head. 'Nope. You weren't wearing much the first time I saw you.'

It was Gabe's turn to blush.

'Not so clever now.' I laughed.

'You're making it up.' Gabe turned the car into Sarah's lane.

'Maybe I am, maybe I'm not,' I said.

Tallulah meowed and scratched the sides of the basket.

'She knows she's home.'

Gabe opened the door of the battered Land Rover.

As I manoeuvred the bulky basket and myself out he held my arm to steady me. I reached over and kissed his cheek. He curled a strand of my hair in his fingers and was gently tugging at it.

We settled Tallulah in and left her with plenty of dried food.

'Let's not go back just yet,' Gabe said. 'Isobel can wait for the shopping. I'll say we got stuck in festival traffic. We need to sort a few things out.'

'It'll be strange to spend some time together in the daylight,' I said with a grin.

We took a throw off the sofa and threw it on the grass in the back garden, then sat down together.

'It's so peaceful here,' I said as I stretched out. 'With the sound of the festival just a faint noise carried on the wind, it's like being safe inside your house with a storm raging outside.'

Gabe lay down next to me and said, 'About last night . . .

it seemed like I was waiting for ever you to come. I'd deliberately arrived a few minutes late. I wanted you to be already there waiting for me. Then when you didn't come part of me was relieved. I convinced myself that my life is complicated enough without having a full-on relationship.'

I moved away from him on the rug. But he moved towards me so that our arms were touching and continued. 'So I wrote the note and left quickly. I couldn't get you out of my head that quickly. The next morning I was coming to find you . . .'

'Jackson is not my boyfriend, you know,' I said.

'You seemed pretty cosy.'

'So do you and Cleo,' I pointed out.

'As Julius would say, touché!'

'Jackson is good-looking and he can be very charming, but he doesn't smell right.'

'What?'

'He doesn't smell of fresh lemon mixed with something deep like freshly dug earth.'

'Yuck!'

'It's the way that you smell to me and I like it,' I said. 'I really like to sniff the side of your cheek.'

Gabe sat up and nuzzled his face next to mine. 'Sniff away.'

'Only if you tell me what I smell of?'

He snuffled round my face and hair. 'Fresh mint with a hint of jasmine.' He sniffed again. 'That might just be sweat.'

'Stop it,' I said, giggling.

Gabe put on a hurt expression. '*You* started the smell thing.'

'How was London?' I asked.

It was like someone had flicked a switch inside Gabe. His face drained of expression and he flopped back down on the rug.

'What is it?' I asked.

'Nothing,' he said, 'and everything . . .'

Then he began to cry. Not snotty loud sobs like mine, but soft straight tears that rolled like trained dancers down his cheek.

We lay in silence for a long time and then I said, 'Meow.'

Gabe smiled. And, wiping away his tears, he said, 'When I was small I used to imagine that I had been abducted by aliens. They had replicated my body and returned a slightly faulty one back to earth. My true body was kept in a large flotation tank full of soft amber jelly where it was warm and safe. The real me was waiting for the aliens to be defeated. My replicate self would then be forced to lie in the tank. I wouldn't want it to be killed. We were all victims of the aliens' fiendish plan. I used to draw endless pictures of aliens and spaceships. I read every book I could find about them. It helped me come to terms with stuff, I suppose.'

I stroked his arm. 'I'm sorry.'

'Look, Jenna. I don't want your pity.'

Gabe pulled his arm away, but I grabbed it back. I said, 'What am I supposed to do? I am sorry that this thing has happened to you. I won't lie. I even feel sorry for myself. That's the truly pathetic thing. I feel sorry for myself. I'm scared.'

'There's nothing to be afraid of,' Gabe said softly.

'Crap! There are heaps of things to be scared of. We are afraid of stuff like snakes and heights for a reason – they can kill us. I'm not scared of you, but I am terrified of the virus inside you!'

'There are risks, that's true, but I would never expose you to any danger. If anything, I'm more at risk from you.'

'What do you mean?'

'My immune system is shot to pieces. Germs that you can shake off could be lethal to me. So many people think that HIV can be cured with a few pills. It can be *controlled* by medication but there is no cure. The bugs can be knocked out, but they can't be killed. If I miss my meds by even an hour, then everything falls apart. The bugs wake up and I have to start all over again. That means more visits to the hospital and tests.'

I stroked his hair. This time he didn't pull away from me.

I said, 'When you are a child you think that everything can be put right. A broken toy can get fixed. A nightlight stops you being scared of the dark. Maybe growing up is realising that life doesn't work out like that. I suppose I've always known, deep down, that Mia would never tell the truth. That our friendship was not as deep as I believe true friendships should be. And I know that your HIV is not going to go away because I'm wishing it. Fairy tales lie. You can't always be rescued.'

'So are you saying that I'm not your handsome prince, come to sweep you off your feet?'

I laughed. 'Just try sweeping me off my feet, mate.'

Gabe lunged at me and we both ended up collapsed on the rug. Neither of us made a move. We just stayed squeezed together for a long time.

'I'm starving,' Gabe said, standing up.

'Crying does that to you,' I said.

He hugged me. 'Tell anyone that you've seen me cry and you are dead meat.'

'No *problemo*. I'll just add it to my list of secrets never to be spoken.'

I hugged Gabe back tightly. I could feel his heart beating fast next to mine.

'Definitely jasmine,' he said, sniffing my cheek again, then followed me into the kitchen.

We were dealing with the situation with jokes. It seemed to work for us.

'Gourmet lunch,' Gabe said as he carried his plate back to the garden.

'*Nouvelle cuisine.*'

We were sharing three crackers with a smear of tuna and a leftover pineapple ring.

'When are you going back to London?' Gabe asked.

'Not sure. Most probably the beginning of September. Why?'

'I am moving back here for a while. I am going to do my A-levels at the community school.'

'One good thing about Mia not spilling the beans is that I still have no school to go to. Nothing definite anyway. Sarah hasn't asked me to leave yet. I'm sure she'd let me stay. I could go to the community school too.'

'That would be good.'

He said it like he really meant it.

'What are Cleo's plans?'

'She's not sure what to do. She is living with her cousin in London during term time, but that is not working out so well. She may hang around here too. You'd be OK with that?'

'Fine.'

What else could I say? I couldn't interfere with the things they shared. I had to accept it.

I rolled over on my front and picked at some of the over-grown grass on the lawn. 'I can't believe we are going to be performing at the festival tomorrow. I've never had any ambition to do that before. I hope I don't freeze when I see everyone.'

'The main thing is not to take it too seriously. Relax and get into the chilled festival mood.'

I sprang to my feet. 'Mum's lent me a great T-shirt to wear. I'll go and get it.'

I raced up to my room and got changed. I was just checking how it looked in the mirror when I felt the hairs on the back of my neck stand on end.

Someone was watching me.

There was only one person who made my flesh creep like that.

'Kai!' I said, without turning round.

Chapter Thirty-Six

'Just can't tear myself away from you, Jenna,' Kai said as he walked into the room. 'Great top, by the way. Classic T-shirts fetch a lot of money these days.'

I leaned against the chest of drawers and said, 'Surely you've taken everything of value by now. That vase must've got you enough.'

'Jenna. Stop being a bread-head. They were only material goods. In the grand scheme of things they don't matter. I'm going through major life changes at the moment.'

There was the sound of a van pulling up outside.

Kai looked away. 'That'll be Emma. I believe you two have met.'

'When you sent her into the shop to check on your record collection,' I said. I thought of Sarah and how much of her life she had sacrificed for him. 'How could you?' I said.

'When you're an adult, you'll understand. Grown-ups play by different rules.'

'It doesn't look very grown-up from where I'm standing.'

Gabe came running up the stairs. 'Everything all right, Jenna?' he asked as his eyes took in the situation.

Kai arched his eyebrows in mock surprise. 'So I'm not the only one having a secret rendez-vous here today.'

'Don't judge everyone by your own low standards. We brought Tallulah back. She'd wandered on to the festival site,' I explained.

'So it takes an hour to bring the cat inside, does it? That's how long I've been waiting up here for you to go.' Kai gave us an annoying grin.

There was a knocking at the door. Kai turned to look.

'You could always help us load some of the furniture into the van,' he said.

'Does Sarah know about this?' I stood beside Gabe and together we blocked the doorway.

'I'm taking my dues here, and then on to the shop.'

Gabe and I looked at each other. We had to do something to stop him.

'We were meaning to tell you . . .' I began.

'But of course you haven't been around,' Gabe added.

Kai's eyes flashed with panic. 'What? Anything happened to my record collection . . . ?'

'No . . . not to your *entire* collection,' Gabe replied, looking at me meaningfully.

'There's still some albums left in the shop, but some aren't there any more,' I said slowly. 'When you sent Emma to snoop in the shop I knew I had to do something.'

'Which ones aren't there?' he asked, his face purple with rage.

Emma continued knocking on the door.

'What did you say?' I pretended I couldn't hear him.

'What have you done with them?' Kai screamed as he grabbed Gabe's T-shirt.

'Leave him alone!' I pulled on his arm.

Emma opened the flap of the letter box and began calling, 'Kai, it's me. Let me in.'

Kai's voice softened. 'OK guys, you've had your fun. Emma is in no condition to be messed around.'

Without speaking, we all turned and walked down the stairs.

I wrenched the door open.

Emma looked surprised and said, 'Oh, we thought you'd be busy at the festival.' She blinked like some kind of sleepy animal.

Gabe glared at her. 'Very convenient time for you to come round and steal Sarah's stuff.'

Emma went up to Kai and took hold of his hand. 'You said it was your stuff.'

'So it is.' He stroked at his chin.

We were all jammed in the hall, but nobody moved.

Emma tugged at Kai's sleeve like a persistent child. 'You said it was all your stuff. That Sarah would give us her blessing. Even let us live in the cottage. Was that a lie?'

'Ssh,' Kai said, a little roughly, as he put a finger to Emma's lips.

'Don't think there will be any more room at the inn once I move in,' I said.

'Now that we can hear ourselves think, let's return to the matter of my records,' Kai said, changing the subject.

'We don't think of them as material goods,' I began.

'We think of them as an insurance policy,' Gabe added.

Kai was getting edgy again. 'Against what?'

'Against any more stuff going walkies from the house – or the shop.'

Kai stroked his chin again. 'I need to know which records are no longer at the shop. They may be ones that can be easily replaced.'

Gabe laughed and shook his head. 'Velvet Fogg is pretty hard to replace and Leafhound is practically impossible.'

Kai's face began to heat up again. 'Where are they?'

'Somewhere safe,' I said.

Chapter Thirty-Seven

After Kai and Emma had left, Gabe and I piled into the Land Rover and raced over to the shop. 'What a team!' Gabe said, laughing.

'We were totally convincing,' I agreed.

'It was like we were reading each other's minds – like we both just knew what to do to rattle Kai.'

I leaped out and opened up the shop. 'Naming those records was inspired.'

We didn't have much time, so we ran to Kai's records and Gabe picked out the really rare ones.

'Where can we hide them?'

'He's bound to come back and look.'

'Yoohoo!' Ava's voice chirped at us from the hairdresser's.

Gabe and I looked at each other and smiled.

When we finally made it back to the festival it was starting to get dark. After leaving the shop, we had to pick up the groceries for the hall. Fortunately Isobel had been sidetracked by a journalist and didn't complain too much about our lateness. Then we had to reassure Sarah that Tallulah was fine and that we had left her enough food. I didn't want to upset her so I didn't mention the Kai and Emma incident.

Mum, Marcus and Aurora were watching a puppet play in the theatre tent. Charlie and Freddie whisked Gabe away to discuss setting up his drum kit.

I decided to go for a look round the festival. By now all three fields designated for camping were jam-packed with an assortment of tents and camper vans. Groups of people sat around eating and drinking. A young woman and an old man started to play their violins together. People started cheering and dancing. It was a beautiful evening.

I found myself smiling privately. For once in my life I felt I was part of something and that the people who mattered liked me for who I was. I wasn't a 'background person' lost in a crowd, or in the foreground only by association. I felt I could handle anything.

Being in Little Netherby – and with Gabe – had given me confidence. Being with Jackson was fun and flattering, but it was like being on shaky ground with him. Besides, I could never respect Jackson again for not standing by me.

I realised that I was very hungry and so I found myself drawn by the food smells to the main field, where the main performing tent and all the food stalls were. I pulled up my hood. There was a slight breeze, and also, I didn't want Sarah to notice me. Despite my hunger, I couldn't face another of her tasteless Soul Food wraps.

I needn't have worried because she was far too busy sitting talking with a group of friends. It was good to see her laughing again. I followed the delicious fried onion smell to the Netherby Farm stall that was selling organic burgers. I bought a large one and sat down on a patch of grass at the side of the stall to enjoy it.

As I was chewing the last mouthful I spotted Mia and her

crew checking out the craft stalls. Mia was striding in front, posing as if she were being filmed. Rebecca and Jackson were a few steps behind. I winced. Not so long ago that would've been me trailing behind and looking grateful to have Mia as a friend. They were laughing, but it was loud attention-seeking laughter and it seemed out of place at the festival. Justin looked uncomfortable and he soon wandered off.

Mia had got me into a lot of trouble lately, but Gabe was right – I'd get over it. And my problem could be fixed. Besides, if I hadn't got into trouble I'd never have been sent to Netherby. I wiped my mouth. I have learned some important things from the experience. Never again would I put myself in the personal assistant role in a friendship. From now on it would be equal terms or nothing. No more making light of bad things and going along with things for the sake of friendship. Friendship should be about standing up for what you believe in and not about being a crowd pleaser. And if you can't forgive your friends their weaknesses, then you should let them go.

Mia and Co were now looking at a clothes stall and were laughing at the goods. Jackson grabbed a feather boa and struck a pose. I found myself smiling at him despite myself. Jackson could always make me smile. After that, they moved on to a stall selling jewellery.

If you hadn't been spying on them as I was, you wouldn't have noticed. I could hardly believe it myself. With one adept movement, Mia took a necklace with one hand and held it up in the air, whilst at the same time slipping a ring into Rebecca's bag. Then they quickly moved on, Mia and Rebecca clinging to each other and giggling. A bemused Jackson followed them. He hadn't seen a thing. Their amusement only lasted a few seconds because a man and a woman quickly surrounded them.

They flashed something that looked like a bus pass at them. Rebecca and Mia froze. Mia offered her handbag up to be searched. She even showed them her purse that must have been full of money.

Everyone looked at them with disgust as they were led away by the plain-clothes police officers.

A discussion followed amongst the crowd about what would happen next:

'Lord Netherby decides whether to press charges or not.'

'They're only a group of kids.'

'But they had money. What about the stallholder?'

'Even if they don't arrest them, they'll have to leave the festival.'

I wandered around in a bit of a daze after that. Memories of the incident with that credit card had come racing back. How Mia had pleaded with me not to say anything. I thought that taking the credit card had been a one-off thing. That we had all been caught up in some mad moment. I never thought for one second that Mia made a habit of it. It wasn't as if she needed the money. How could I have got someone so wrong?

A loud horn sounded in my ear. I jumped. I was standing next to a stilt-walking clown.

'Cheer up!' He honked the horn in my face again.

I faked a smile and walked away as fast as I could.

Without realising it, I had walked into the theatre field. In front of me was a small striped tent. There were ripples of laughter, which were followed by loud clapping. I popped my head round the flap and was hit by a wall of heat. The small tent was packed and a puppet play was in full swing. Right at the front I could see Aurora sitting next to Mum. Marcus was asleep in her lap. Mum was rocking him whilst laughing at the show.

How Marcus could sleep through all that din was beyond me.

I felt a huge wave of affection flood over me. I know that I had disappointed Mum, but now was the time to make it up to her. The summer was practically over and plans needed to be made. I had a direction for my life. I decided I was going to school here in Netherby, where I would work really hard and be a credit to Mum.

An image flashed into my head of Gabe and me sitting in a café studying together. We'd go to the observatory at Greenwich and stand with one foot in the Eastern Hemisphere and one in the Western Hemisphere just like everybody else. I was looking forward to doing lots of things with Gabe.

As I was heading back to our bit of campsite I went past the 'Alternative Zone'. There was a large bonfire in the centre and people were gathered round banging drums and chanting.

Drawn by the heat of the fire I went in. I sat down as close to the fire as I could get without drawing attention to myself. I found a smooth flat stone to sit on.

Nothing in particular seemed to be happening. Some people were giving massages. A woman was casting stones on the ground like dice and speaking to someone. I suppose it was some kind of fortune-telling.

'Jump in my grave just as quickly,' a voice said next to me and I looked up to see a tall woman dressed in a long woollen cloak.

'Sorry.' I stood up. 'I didn't realise it was your place.'

'Stay there,' she said, then she chuckled. 'Don't mind me. My name is Cassiopeia, Cassie for short, and I'm just a grumpy old crone.'

She sat down beside me. The air around us filled with her sickly rich perfume. I was desperate to get away, but didn't want to hurt her feelings.

'Like the constellation,' I said, thinking Gabe would be proud of me for remembering.

'I expect you've come for the healing circle. It should have started by now, but things always run late. That's hippies for you.' She chuckled again.

'No, I haven't come to the healing circle. I was just wandering about the place.'

'So you were summoned, then.' She turned and looked very closely at me. 'You have a good, strong soul.' She tapped the stone I was sitting on. 'You found the healing stone. You have come to heal someone you love.'

An image of Gabe jumped into my head.

Cassie nodded. 'The boy. I can feel his pain.'

I shuddered. I was sure she was just taking a wild guess and got lucky. But all the same, it freaked me out and I looked around for a way to escape, but more and more people had sat around and I was hemmed in.

I resigned myself to staying. A healing circle couldn't hurt, could it?

Chapter Thirty-Eight

We all had to stand up and form a circle around the fire. There must have been about a hundred people there. Cassie hurled some incense on the fire. The drummer began a low, mournful beat as we were told to face up to the pain that was in our lives. I imagined Gabe's bugs in the blood and I began to move around the circle stomping on them and shouting at them to go away.

Someone began to play on a flute and someone else joined in with some jangling Indian bells and, as the rhythm changed, we were encouraged to embrace the pain and bathe it in a golden light. I held out my hand and imagined a little bug sitting on my hand. I bathed it in golden light that was sticky like honey. The bug enjoyed this and stayed there frozen in the honey that began to harden. Now that it was trapped it couldn't hurt anyone.

Then everyone swirled around the circle. It was like country dancing gone mad. I was picked up and twirled around.

Someone tapped me on the shoulder and said in a grand voice, 'May I have the honour of the next dance?'

At first I thought it was Julius, but it wasn't.

It was Gabe. 'Didn't have you down as a hippy chick,' he said, grinning.

I checked to see if Cleo was around. She'd probably have something sneery to say. But Gabe was alone.

'I missed you,' he said and kissed the top of my head. He puckered up his face. 'Yuck. You're sweaty and taste funny.'

I laughed. 'It must be the incense from the fire.'

He put his arm around me and said, 'Come on. I've been preparing a surprise for you.'

I stood still and pretended to pout. 'But I might not want to leave the healing circle.'

'Is that what it is? Well, I think you can leave now – you look healed enough. I thought we'd spend some time alone together before things get really crazy.'

As I was leaving the field, Cassie ran up to me, pressed something into my hand and hugged me, saying, 'Be strong, Jenna.'

I put the stone in my jacket pocket and smiled at her.

Chapter Thirty-Nine

We left the field where the festival was and made our way back towards the hall. Gabe covered my eyes with his hands and led me down a path. My feet slipped on a patch of wet grass, but Gabe steadied me.

'Surprise!' he said.

It was amazing. The grotto was bathed in pink-and-green spotlights. Water poured from Neptune's mouth.

'One of the perks of being a lord's son is that you get to play in the grounds,' he said.

I was still standing there, open-mouthed, as Gabe went on. 'For my next trick . . .' he spread his arms wide like a cheesy magician and ran towards the Greek temple. A few seconds later it was all lit up with fairy lights.

'Christmas has come early,' I said, laughing as I joined Gabe on a tartan rug piled up with cushions. Beside him were a battered old wicker basket and his telescope.

'I wanted to grab some time alone with you. Can you stay for a while?' he said.

'This is truly amazing. There's no need to worry about being late. I'm supposed to be staying in the tent with the rest of the band tonight,' I said.

'I'd better switch off the lights now.' Gabe began to light

several candles. 'Otherwise, Dad will give me a hard time about wasting electricity.'

I grinned as Gabe opened the basket and took out a bottle. 'Another one of the perks of being the son of a lord.'

'Champagne?' I said.

'Non-alcoholic peach fizz – it was all I could find, but we can pretend.' Gabe popped the cork and tipped the drink into two old-fashioned glasses.

'We don't have champagne in the house. Dad is the poorest person I know. Money's always a big issue in our house. The upkeep of Netherby Hall costs a fortune, plus he gives most of the profits from the festival away to charity.'

'Same in ours. Mum had to buy an expensive house so that I could go to a good school and mix with motivated and well-adjusted children who would get me excluded. Which reminds me . . .'

I went on to tell him all about Mia's little shoplifting spree. 'I wonder what's happening to them now.'

Gabe stretched out on the rug. 'That's easy. They're at the house. Rebecca was boohooing like a baby. Mia was acting the innocent. The stallholder was glad to get his stuff back and wanted to get back to his stall. The police were dealing with another incident. So Dad phoned their parents and put on his best Lord Netherby voice and asked them to come and collect their children at once. They are going to spend the night in the guest room.'

I sighed bitterly. 'So no police means Mia's got away with it again. She can twist her parents around her little finger.'

'I'm not so sure. People like her do get caught out in the end.'

'No, they don't. When is Kai going to get what's coming to

him? It's not fair . . .' I said and frowned. 'And don't tell me life is not fair.'

'Would you like to swap places with Kai or Mia for one second?' Gabe looked quite serious. 'Could you bear to be as morally empty as them?'

'It might be fun for a while. I'm sure I could write some better poetry and I'd be nicer to Sarah than the real Kai is. It'd be fun rifling through Mia's wardrobe. But, hang on – they'd be in my body at the same time. No way. I couldn't bear Mia being me even for a second.'

'Being strong in yourself is the best defence against people like that,' Gabe said.

'That's what the old hippy lady told me. She said to be strong. I wish I hadn't given in to Mia so many times just for a quiet life. But Sarah really, really loves Kai.'

'He doesn't pay her back with love, does he?' Gabe said.

'Maybe she just needs him,' I added as a picture of Cleo jumped unwelcome into my mind. I knew that Cleo desperately needed Gabe's friendship.

'He despises her, but he needs her at the same time. That's not love.'

'He's got Emma and the baby coming,' I said.

Gabe shook his head. 'Wonder how his character will stand up to that test?'

I finished off my drink and stretched my arms. 'My, aren't you and I so mature and wise? If only people would listen to us.'

Gabe laughed. 'Let's look at something really old and wise.' He reached for his telescope and positioned it north.

I hugged my knees close to my chest and looked up. I took a deep breath, filled my lungs with the sweet air and became absorbed in the landscape of the sky. I rested one hand in the small of Gabe's back as I continued looking upwards.

I felt something that I'd never felt before. It was a feeling beyond happiness and very close to sadness. A feeling so powerful it would have to fade soon or I'd burst. I felt this way because I was with Gabe.

This wasn't a fairy tale. It was more precious than that. Gabe had given me the option to walk away and even though it was scary I had chosen not to. I was trusting my own feelings and I felt proud of myself. Because it was a hard choice and we had faced up to it we had earned this perfect moment and every other perfect moment that came afterwards.

We understood and liked each other. I knew we could support each other. I was looking forward to finding out more things about him. I was looking forward to sharing more experiences with him. Gabe took his eye away from the telescope.

'A perfect night sky. You can even see Cassiopeia.'

I felt a tingle down my spine as I recalled my meeting with Cassie and how she'd told me to be strong.

I squinted into the telescope and followed Gabe's instructions.

'Can you see it yet? It's a very distinctive group. There are five main stars. The ones like a letter W.'

'I've got it!'

'And I've got you, Jenna. You don't know what that means to me.'

Gabe grabbed hold of my hand. I squeezed it back and said, 'You big softie.'

We lay together for a long while holding each other and not speaking. I took in Gabe's wonderful smell and rested my head on his chest, feeling his heart beating. My throat felt dry. Every sense and feeling in my body was heightened. I slipped my hand underneath his T-shirt and felt his skin. It felt warm and soft.

Then I was overcome by the biggest fit of giggles.

'What is it?' Gabe looked puzzled.

'I was just remembering the first time I saw you. You were sitting in a deck chair at Charlie's place and you were stroking your chest like I am now. I couldn't take my eyes off you. It seems funny that so much has happened since then.'

'You're crazy, Jenna. But I love you anyway.'

Gabe spoke those words so quietly that I half thought I'd imagined it. The weight of Gabe's feelings behind those three clichéd words hung in the air for us both to feel. He'd told me he'd loved me before in his letter, but this was the first time he'd said it out loud. I considered saying them back to him, but stopped myself. There was no rush. There would be plenty of time for me to tell him how I felt. We were going to go to school together.

For the moment it was enough to be together falling asleep in a Greek temple, looking at the stars.

Chapter Forty

A large crow screeching overhead woke me up the next morning. There was no sign of Gabe, only a note saying he had gone to get us coffee. I don't think I'd ever been awake so early. Not since I was a baby. I pulled my fleece on and stood up to get warm. My whole body felt charged with electricity.

It was a new day and a new beginning for me. Something inside me had shifted. It was like I was seeing things clearly for the first time in ages. I knew where I stood with Mia and Jackson and I knew where I wanted to be – with Gabe. As I put my hands in my fleece to keep warm I felt the stone from Cassie. When I looked at it in the daylight I saw it was a piece of amber with a tiny insect trapped inside. I stroked the stone and put it back in my pocket.

Gabe came back with a battered thermos and two chipped mugs.

'It's pandemonium back at the ranch,' Gabe said. 'Mia and Rebecca stayed in the guest room. Rebecca's parents have arrived and they're none too pleased.'

I shrugged my shoulders. 'You mistake me for someone who cares.'

Gabe poured the coffee into the mugs.

'Not even if your name was mentioned?' he added.

'They can't pin this one on me,' I said, shaking my head.

'Rebecca told her mum about the ring being slipped into her bag. She said, "This is what must have happened to poor Jenna".'

'There's nothing poor about me!' I snapped back. 'If Rebecca says that's what happened, then she'll be believed. Her mum is the chair of the school governors, after all. She was the one who recommended that I make a "fresh start" somewhere else.'

Gabe prodded me in the shoulder and said, 'So you don't want to hear about what happened when Mia's mum arrived, then . . . ?'

My ears pricked up at that. I cupped the mug in my hands and said, 'Tell me everything.'

Before he could say a word there was a loud rustling noise and Aurora burst through the bushes, saying, 'You've missed a right bloody ding-dong.'

Gabe and I both chanted, 'Language, Aurora!'

She squeezed herself between us and said excitedly, 'After you sneaked off with the flask, it was like a courtroom drama. As soon as she saw them, she burst into floods and started saying she was being victimised.' Aurora's eyes flashed as she recounted every part.

Gabe and I smiled at each other.

'Rebecca's mother said her daughter had never been in trouble before she linked up with Mia. Mia answered back, "They didn't find a thing on me. Just like last time. Nothing on me."

'Rebecca's mum went very pale and said, "So this has nothing to do with truth and everything to do with what you can get away with." Mia sniggered. So did her dad. That was too much for our dad, Gabe.'

Aurora stood up and mimicked Lord Netherby. 'Your

attitude is despicable and goes some way to explaining your daughter's lax morality. I had informed the police that I would be dropping the charges, but I am tempted to change my mind. There is a witness to the theft. The man who runs the burger stall will, I'm sure, make a statement that he saw one girl slip the ring into the other's bag. May I also add, on another matter, that Jenna Hudson is a personal friend of this family and I have found her to be a decent person. I am also considering writing to your school to reopen that case. I am not without influence. There is probably CCTV footage in the area of the shop.'

'That was my idea!' Gabe piped up. 'Dad and Isobel had heard about your exclusion and I put them right – I hope you don't mind.'

So Gabe had been planning ways to help me out. If it were Jackson, he would never have troubled himself to do that! Gabe was not the type to walk away from a situation.

Aurora waved her arms at us impatiently. 'I haven't finished! When they heard this, Mia began to cry and whimper, "I didn't mean to do it. I couldn't help myself. No one stopped me. Jenna and Jackson egged me on."

'Mia's dad offered to pay everybody off, but Dad said there was a principle at stake, and unless Mia formally admitted to the school that she had used the credit card then he would press charges.'

Aurora cheered and Gabe grinned.

I surprised myself about how deflated I felt. Hadn't I been waiting for weeks for this to happen?

As I was gathering together my stuff and helping Gabe tidy up Aurora said, 'How is Marcus today? He wasn't feeling very well yesterday.'

'He's probably just over excited,' I said. Nothing was going to spoil my day.

Or so I thought.

Although it was still really early, lots of people were up and about queuing for the showers and toilets. Some people were still playing music. A helicopter flew overhead, bringing in one of the bands.

And I was going to be part of it! In years to come I could say I performed at the Netherby Festival.

Sarah had said that I could drop in any time and use the small washroom in her caravan, so I went round to the side and tapped on the door. No answer. I tapped again and listened. I thought I could hear a faint sob.

'Sarah, are you all right?' I said as I let myself in.

Someone was sitting next to her on the small seat. As I walked in I overheard him saying, 'Kai is really sorry that he hurt his special sad-eyed lady.' He was stroking Sarah's hair and she was letting him. They both turned to look at me.

'I just came round for a wash, like you said I could.'

Sarah looked up at me. Through her tears, her eyes were shining.

'Jenna! You can be the first one to hear our news.'

'Sarah, are you sure?' Kai looked a little shifty.

'I want the world to know that we are back together again.' Sarah flung her arms round his neck. 'Life has been such a torment without you, Kai.'

Kai looked down at his feet and mumbled, ' Sarah and I are back together. I'm coming back to the shop and to the cottage.'

'What about Emma?' the words tumbled out of my mouth before my common sense could put a stop to them.

Sarah's eyes darkened. 'We are not going to dwell on the mistakes of the past. This is a new beginning. There will be no blame.'

Kai hugged her. 'That's my beautiful lady! I was entranced by a siren who poisoned my body, but my heart was always true to you.'

It was too sickening to watch. As I turned to go, I said bitterly, 'Is that baby just a mistake you are not going to dwell on?'

I slammed the door shut on my way out.

Chapter Forty-One

I stomped blindly out of the caravan. How could Sarah be so stupid as to fall for Kai's lines? How could she gloss over the 'small matter' of a baby?

I didn't see Ava until it was too late and I'd bumped into her.

'I'm sorry, I didn't mean to knock you over.'

She patted her hairdo back into place. 'That's all right, dear. I was just taking some lemon drizzle cake to Julius. He forgets to eat, you know.'

Ava gripped my arm and studied me for a moment. 'But who's rained on your parade? Had a tiff with lover boy?' she said and winked.

'Just bumped into Kai and Sarah, if you must know.'

'So they have kissed and made up. I love a happy ending. Will you be wanting those records back, then?' she cooed.

'I know at least two people who won't think that this is a happy ending.'

I told her all about Emma and the baby she was expecting. Ava went pale and crumpled a little. She leaned against a tree for support.

I felt terrible. 'I didn't mean to upset you. I'm just feeling so angry. I didn't think about how you might react.'

Ava smiled. 'I'm not shocked. It just brought some painful memories flooding back, that's all.'

She was shaking.

'I'm sorry, Ava. Can I help?'

'You're forty-four years too late to help me out . . . Sixteen years old . . . I can still see myself so clearly. Thought I knew it all. Didn't know enough to stop myself getting pregnant, did I? It was a big deal in those days. I'm sure the boy would have stood by me, but he was off to university. Had big dreams to become a writer. I was just a summer fling to him. My parents could've disowned me, but they packed me off to a mother-and-baby hostel, where I got to hold my son for ten minutes before they took him away from me.' She wiped her eye. 'It was for the best. I couldn't afford to keep him. A family adopted him and I had to carry on with my hairdressing apprenticeship. It wasn't done to keep in touch in those days.'

She pulled out a crumpled tissue from the sleeve of her cardigan and blew loudly. I hugged her. She hugged me back.

'Now, about those records. Didn't you say they're worth a lot of money?'

I nodded. 'Gabe said they were extremely rare.' I loved just saying his name.

'I'll see they get passed on to the right person,' Ava said.

By the time I got back to the tent, the rehearsal had started. Charlie was busy working himself up into a state of nervous tension. Gabe was trying his best to improvise a set of drums on a tabletop.

Cleo was huddled in a corner, looking miserable. Freddie had written out a play list that was passed around.

Charlie announced, 'There's been another development. We couldn't find you or Gabe last night to tell you. Lyle

Hasslett, the lead singer from the Stale Pumpkins, has decided to make an appearance at the festival after all, so we have been cut to three songs.'

'That's not in the spirit of anti-folk, is it?' I asked.

'It's not his fault. It's his PR people. They think he can be a crossover act,' Charlie said quickly.

'Sounds painful,' I joked.

Freddie giggled.

Charlie frowned. 'It means that we've had to cut a few songs, including "Because the Night".'

I felt a huge pang of disappointment. Suddenly I became aware of everybody's eyes on me waiting for a reaction.

I covered my face. 'Stop looking at me! I'll get over it.'

Gabe laughed. 'Call yourself a diva? You should have thrown a hissy-fit by now.'

I gave an exaggerated shrug. 'It's only the Netherby Festival, the largest showcase of alternative music in the country. No *problemo*.' Then I began to fake a screaming fit. Even Cleo had to smile. That had to be worth something.

There were a few hours to go before the performance and I badly needed to come into contact with some hot water. I also needed to check up on Mum and Marcus. So I took off back to the cottage.

It turned out that Marcus really was sick. He was running a temperature, so Mum had decided to phone for a doctor. He was asleep when I got back.

'Marcus has got chicken pox,' Mum said. 'He'll be sick for a couple of weeks and then he'll be fine.'

It felt weird being alone with Mum in Sarah's place. Mum belonged in a tidy clutter-free kitchen with a stocked fridge. It was strange watching her drink tea from a chipped mug that in our house would have been smashed and used to line plant pots weeks ago.

'I've missed having you around the place,' Mum said.

'No one to moan at,' I said, rolling my eyes.

'No one to drain my wallet or complain about my cooking.'

'After staying with Sarah, I'll never do *that* again. There's only so many things you can do with a tin of tuna.'

Mum laughed. 'She always was a terrible cook.'

'You do know that Kai has come crawling back to her.'

I told her what I had witnessed in the caravan.

'If it makes Sarah happy, then I'm not going to criticise.' Mum fixed me with one of her stares. 'Besides, she's worked wonders with you.'

'You mean I'm speaking again.' I stuck my tongue out.

'You look different, seem more confident. I can't explain it. I suppose you've grown up a bit.'

I took a deep breath. I was dying to tell her all about my summer and about Gabe. But I knew that it wasn't the right time.

'I'd like to make a fresh start here, Mum. There's a great local school and I will be sixteen in September. I can work in the bookshop or at the café. If Kai won't let me stay here, then I'm sure I could find a cheap flat. I've got lots of friends around here that will look out for me . . . Please.'

Mum took lots of sips from her tea before she said, 'Are you sure you won't get homesick? I had arranged a place for you at another school in London.'

'Of course I will, but you and Marcus can visit lots and I can come up to London. I know that I can make a go of things here.'

'I'll give it some serious thought, but I need you to be

honest with me about that credit card business.'

So I was. It seemed so inconsequential to me now. I even told her about Rebecca and the ring and I told her about what Lord Netherby had done.

Mum leaped up from her chair. 'I'm going to get on that phone and make Mrs Kelly take you back.'

'Don't do that, Mum. Like I said, I'm not sure I want to go back there anyway.'

I let Mum seethe for a while and groan on about how bad everyone at the school had made her feel and how sorry they were going to be. She finished off her tea and slammed the mug down on the table, saying, 'I always thought that Mia would be at the bottom of it.'

'So don't send me to a school that is populated by Mias, then! I don't want to go back to a place that's obsessed with exam results and where I have to feel so grateful for being allowed into in the first place, because I'm not quite rich or clever enough. I want to go to a place that values me and my strengths.'

Mum stared at me for a long time before saying in a soft voice, 'Wow! You really have grown up.'

'Don't be fooled. I'd still kill for chocolate.' I started to sing our 'Must Have Chocolate Now' song.

Mum laughed and took out a large bar from her handbag. We polished it off between us before it was time to start getting ready for the performance.

I soaked in the bath for a long time. I wanted to feel good for tonight.

If only I'd known then how fast things were unravelling as I lay soaking and dreaming.

Chapter Forty-Two

My head was buzzing with the excitement and my stomach churned with nerves. The reality of performing at the festival was starting to bite, even though I was only singing back-up now. I spent ages drying my hair and going over the songs in my head. Mum had washed the Patti Smith T-shirt. I put it on carefully.

When I came downstairs, Gabe was in the lounge. Tallulah was sitting on his lap. There was something about the expression on his face that bothered me. He was trying too hard to look as if nothing was the matter.

'Mum didn't say that you were here,' I said, frowning.

'She's upstairs with Marcus. I said I'd wait until you were ready. You look great.'

'Gabe, what is it?'

Tallulah jumped from his lap and hid under the sofa.

Gabe took me in his arms and said, 'It's Cleo. She's really sick. After you left she collapsed. We had to call an ambulance.'

'What is it?'

'They're not sure, but her immune system is shot to pieces. Turns out that she hadn't been taking her meds on time. She's got a raging temperature and is really sick. Later tonight, when she's stable, they're probably going to transfer her to a London hospital.'

I remembered about Marcus.

'Gabe, get out of this house now! Go.' I pushed him out of the door. We walked across the road to the space by the wall where Gabe always waited for me.

'It's Marcus. He's got chicken pox. Cleo spent a lot of time with him the other day,' I explained.

Gabe's eyes narrowed. 'That can be really nasty. I'm going to go up to London after the gig tonight.'

'I'll come with you. It'll be all right, I've had chicken pox.' I touched his arm.

Gabe pulled away from me. 'No, Jenna.'

'I'll come up tomorrow, then,' I said. Gabe's coldness was frightening me.

Gabe said slowly, 'I want you to stay away.'

'I won't get in the way. We can meet up for coffee after you've checked up on Cleo.'

'No way, Jenna. This has got to stop now.'

Then the meaning of his words hit me. 'So last night was a joke, was it?' Hot tears filled my eyes.

Gabe said nothing.

'Speak to me!' I screeched.

'I meant everything I said last night . . .'

'Why do I feel that there is a "but" coming?'

'Don't make things any harder than they already are, Jenna.'

'I'll make things as hard as I can to make you stay.'

'You're sounding like Sarah now. Trying to cling on.'

'That was below the belt, Gabe,' I whispered as I leaned against the wall for support. 'Hit me in my stomach as well as my heart.'

Gabe turned away and began to pace around in small, agitated circles.

'I've never felt this way about a person before, Jenna. You're special to me. We sort of fit together. That's how it feels to me.'

'Gabe, I feel it too.'

'Cleo needs me more than you do right now.'

'But we can't be apart.'

'Cleo has nobody. Her mum and dad are gone. Everyone else in her family had rejected her apart from one cousin who lets her stay with her out of "duty" and so long as she never tells anyone about her HIV status. I promised Mum that I'd always look out for Cleo. She has always looked out for me.'

'What about the group that you go to? Can't they help her?'

'It's a lifeline for both of us. Somewhere we go where we don't have to check ourselves every five minutes. Where people understand. But it's not enough.'

'I understand.'

'You try, Jenna.'

'I'm trying now. I really am. I'm not asking you to stop being friends with Cleo.'

'I need to put Cleo first in my life at the moment. It's the right thing to do. This isn't a game. Her health depends on it.'

'So we have to stop seeing each other? It doesn't make sense.'

'We need to be apart. There are things I have to do . . .'

I swallowed. Gabe had to stand by Cleo and keep his promises to his Mum and Cleo's. Even though he didn't love Cleo in the same way, he still had to be there for her. She needed him more. I swallowed again. Deep down I knew that what he was saying was right.

It hurt so much to think about it . . .

My brain whizzed, searching for ways round this.

'How long? A few days, weeks or what?'

'We can't tie ourselves down with false promises.' Gabe's voice cracked.

'Can we stay in touch?' I felt all fierce inside like a wild animal fighting to the death to save her cub. If only I could write and e-mail Gabe, then I knew that I could win him over.

'Cleo has to believe that it is over between us. Otherwise she wouldn't let me look after her. She needs me.'

'*I* need you too,' I whimpered.

'No, you don't.' Gabe looked away. 'You can't need me. This is too difficult for me to handle. I've been selfish, Jenna. You have to make your own way in the world. Besides, it's not just about Cleo.'

'So you're using her illness as an excuse, then?' I flared up.

'No, but Cleo falling sick has made me think again about us. It's not fair on you, Jenna.'

'I'm a big girl and I want to be with you. You've explained some of the risks and I can learn more as we go along. I love you.' I grabbed his face with my hand and turned it towards me.

He looked away. 'It's because I love you, Jenna, that I can't see you for a while. I don't want you to have to deal with it if I get really sick. You're too young. You need some breathing space. I'm not sure if I'm ready to deal with a relationship. The closeness frightens me. The thought of what might happen . . .'

'So, you're walking out on me.'

'I'm going to Italy with Cleo. Dad's cousin has a villa there and I think the climate will help her. I was thinking about doing this before I met you.' Gabe's voice was cold and firm.

'I couldn't bear not to have any contact with you for all that time,' I said. 'It hurts even to think about it.'

'Every year on the Saturday of the August bank holiday at

ten p.m., look up at the sky. Cassiopeia should be there in the north. I will do the same.'

The pain of losing Gabe was so unbearable that all I could say was, 'See you, then,' and I marched back into the cottage without looking back. There was nothing that I could do or say that could change the situation.

I spent the next hour in my bedroom crying my eyes out.

Mum left me well alone.

The crying wore me out and numbed the pain for a while. Was this Gabe's way of dumping me? Telling me that we could have to wait years. He might not be alive in two or three years' time . . .

I couldn't bear that thought. No. I knew he loved me. Cleo's latest illness had shaken him up and he had decided to do the noble thing by me – and Cleo. He was going to keep his promise to his mother and stand by Cleo and support her through a difficult time. He was probably trying to do what he thought was the right thing by me in leaving me. Maybe we both needed some more growing-up time.

I loved him even more for that. He was taking responsibility for someone and keeping a promise that he had made. It was a promise that needed to be kept. Not like the kind of promises that people like Mia held you to. Or the shallow promises that people like Kai made and broke every few seconds.

What sort of relationship could we have in the future if he didn't support Cleo now? I would just have to learn to deal with the pain of being apart from someone that I loved.

But there was just one last thing to do.

Let Gabriel know how much I loved him.

Chapter Forty-Three

As soon as we walked out on to the stage a camera began snapping and flashing at us like we were superstars. It didn't matter that it was only Julius.

Ava waved at us from the front row. 'Yoohoo!'

Mum was sitting next to her (Muriel had agreed to babysit Marcus). Even Sarah was there. Thankfully there was no sign of Kai.

I'd like to say we were wonderful, but we were patchy with some good bits.

That's the good thing about anti-folk music. It's not about being slick, it's about communicating. At least that's what Charlie was always banging on about. Gabe was a little off the beat from time to time and my eyes were puffy and my voice was shaky.

Lyle was getting all twitchy as he stood in the wings surrounded by his people.

I walked centre stage and said, 'I know Lyle is itching to get on and you're dying to see him, but I'd just like to do one more song. It's called "Because the Night", and the person it is dedicated to knows who they he is.'

I caught the band on the hop. Freddie was already off-stage, so I just began to sing. As I sang I rolled all my feelings in my stomach into a ball of emotion and then let them out. I forgot about the audience. I just let rip.

I wanted Gabe to know how much he meant to me.

. . . Because the night belongs to love . . .

When I finished singing there was a pause.

I've made a right fool of myself, I thought as I felt myself shrinking.

Then Gabe grabbed me and kissed me onstage in front of everyone.

There was a loud cheer. The camera flashed. Even Lyle walked on stage to bathe in some of our glory.

I held on to Gabe. There was nothing left to say. All I could do was hold on to him for one last time. It didn't matter that there were hundreds of people watching me.

That kiss was going to have to last me for a long time.

Epilogue

Mum thought I was crazy when I asked for a telescope for Christmas and the neighbours probably think I'm a pervert when they see me stargazing. But this is London and no one says anything.

I completely agree with Plato. Astronomy *does* compel us to look upwards and towards another world. I love the night sky. Looking upwards raises your spirits. I always feel more hopeful when I'm looking at the stars.

Even in London, on a clear night, you can see stars. There are so many constellations with fantastic names like Ursa Major, Corona Borealis and Aquila.

I managed eventually, after a lot of squinting and false starts, to find Cassiopeia.

I wish more people would understand that there is no time limit on growing up. Some people can be mature at sixteen and some people act like spoiled children all of their lives. Kai and Sarah were supposed to be the adults, but look how they behaved.

There's also no age limit for finding your true love. Just because I was fifteen when I met Gabe it doesn't mean that our feelings weren't real or that we couldn't do the right thing – no matter how much it hurt.

Loving Gabe taught me so much. To learn from my mistakes and to forgive the mistakes that other people have made. I'm not afraid to stand up for what I believe in and don't feel the need to follow the crowd. I'm not a background person any more.

When I look at the night sky I feel close to Gabriel.

Tonight I feel especially close to him because I know that, wherever he is, he's looking at Cassiopeia and he's thinking of me.

Acknowledgements

With thanks to Alishia for listening to this story and giving
me great advice and support. To James for introducing
me to anti-folk music and to The BaSe and
TEEN SPIRIT at Body & Soul.

To find out more about Body & Soul,
visit their website at www.bodyandsoul.demon.co.uk